Game Point

Malcolm Hollingdrake

First published in 2017 by Bloodhound Books

www.bloodhoundbooks.com

ISBN: 978-1-912175-12-3

Also available in the DCI Bennett Harrogate Crime Series

Only The Dead
Hell's Gate
Flesh Evidence

For
Sheila Hollingdrake
Moira Walsh
and
Nancy Doherty

The Dewar sisters

In Memory of
David William Hollingdrake
12/01/1952 - 10/01/2017

"There are moments when I feel that the Shylocks, the Judases, and even the Devil are broken spokes in the great wheel of good which shall in due time be made whole."

Helen Keller (1880-1968)

Prologue

May, 2017

Cyril never thought he would return to the café, *La Cigogne,* nor to the beautiful town of Munster, set in the Haut-Rhin department of France, but here he was again. He had promised himself never to return but owing to his recent experiences, he had been drawn there, not pulled kicking and screaming, but seduced by his memories of its stunning beauty, its quiet and of course, its wine. If you were planning to drink to forget, then you could be in no better place to receive the offerings from Bacchus, for forget he must or he knew that he was finished professionally.

The café offered a moment's respite from a busy morning's walk; his hangover had cleared slowly leaving only a hunger for a late morning meal. He stared out across the square as the traffic flowed past, some vehicles rumbling along the ancient cobbles whilst others ran more quietly along the smooth tarmac. Each individual sound rekindled a memory, opened a window to the last occasion he had sat at this spot. He looked up onto the stacks of twigs and branches perched high on the towering chimneystacks of the council offices, the empty nests a sharp reminder of his personal loss. Ironically, the storks would return in the early summer, a legal transit from the African continent.

The last time he had been there it had been so different in many ways, the weather kinder and the traffic heavier. The constant rattle had competed with the continuous clattering of the storks' beaks high in their branch-filled, chimney-top nests. He remembered that the cacophony seemed to bring a certain contentment, where the natural world and that created by man over the centuries amalgamated somehow into a tranquil harmony.

The sound of a car horn brought him briefly back to the present. He wrapped his scarf a little more tightly and relaxed, helped by the e-cigarette held between his lips. He closed his eyes and visualised the storks, long of limb, as they flew in majestic circles from high above before alighting on their branch-woven nests on what appeared to be dislocated knees, ready to regurgitate their stomach contents to their young's ever pleading, wide-open beaks.

He shuffled his feet with an unease that could only come from a man entrapped in an inner guilt and regret. He casually moved the remaining piece of flammekueche onto his fork; the Munster cheese, onion and small pieces of bacon tasted wonderful. He followed it with a sip of Alsace white wine whilst glancing across the Place du Marché and towards the church, its towering walls dwarfing the buildings to its right. He checked the clock against his watch as he always did with any clock he saw. He had been there an hour. It was the fifth day of his compulsory holiday, his prescribed and ordered rest. Probably, if he were to be honest, this was why he had returned to the security of the past, to a place he knew so well before it had happened; it was his way of protesting against himself, it was his way of purging the memory of recent events whilst needing the security of familiarity.

It was the sudden speed of the movement that caught the extremity of his peripheral vision, waking his brain from the shadows of the recent past. The hawk swooped diagonally from high to low across the stone façade of the church building before crashing into its victim, an unsuspecting pigeon that had just left the security of a high ledge. There was a natural explosion resulting in myriad loose, grey and white feathers that cascaded like unwanted confetti in front of the church and onto the steps. The cruelty of nature made Cyril focus on the fine, fluttering feathers, each holding his attention until they all came to rest. As the final feather fell, his memory started to replay the last few difficult months… he'd never lost a colleague before. His mind invoked the once significant and unwelcome receipt of a white feather and he shuddered. He knew everyone had done what was humanly possible, no one had stood back; there was only bravery and professionalism but that hadn't been enough. He had played the final incidents of the case over and over again and each time a small part of him crumbled and died.

Chapter One

June, 2016

The breathing increased to accompany the ethereal moans and animalistic grunts that grew louder as the firm hips pounded frantically against the soft flesh of the folded female, enthusiastically bent and stretched over the wooden table. She wore nothing apart from a Venetian mask, decorated with curled playing cards forming a crown and an elaborate collar, the gilded lips preserved in a permanent smile. Her long fingers curled and grasped at the far edge of the table top, her back slightly arched to allow maximum penetration. Oil or perspiration glistened along the length of her body, reflecting the bright lights from above. Suddenly the thrusting stopped. A hand leaned forward and grasped her neck before pulling her upright and to her feet. Quickly, strong hands dropped to her shoulders before urgently guiding her body round whilst at the same time pushing her down to her knees. One hand went swiftly to remove the mask and obediently she opened her mouth.

The neon light on the tripod-held camera, continued to blink bright blue.

Chapter Two

Late September, 2016

It was a fitting end to a miserable day as Mother Nature forced fine needles of icy rain into the exposed flesh of Cyril Bennett's neck. He quickened his pace as he turned down Belford Street, but here, the wind seemed even more determined to aggravate, whipping the biting rain more strongly as it funnelled its full force between the buildings. Feeling beaten into submission, he stopped before slipping the auction-house catalogue he had just collected inside his overcoat. He defiantly turned up his coat collar before glancing at the clock on the Rogers' Almshouses' tower; he checked his watch, shook his wrist and checked the watch again. It was four-thirty and already the evening was drawing in, helped by the intensity of the low, smothering, overcast sky. '*Winter's just around the corner,*' he thought. How he loathed the impending dark, winter days and with them, the increased criminality that always seemed to go hand in protective glove.

Cyril's eyes reviewed the vertical stone tower from the clock before they came to rest on the carved bust of the building's benefactor, a long dead, Bradford merchant, George Rogers. The green-tinged, sculpted features stared blindly back, oblivious to the forces the weather had thrown over many years. Cyril's eyes fell further until they reached the intricately carved stonework depicting a wicker beehive. It had always been a symbol of industry for Rogers, an industry that had been the source of his considerable wealth.

Further chills ran down the nape of Cyril's neck but this time it was not the cold, it was the image. It brought to mind a confusing and distasteful police investigation that had been wrapped up not too long ago. As a consequence, he had never touched honey since; for him its sweet taste was now sullied, it represented evil. He inhaled the menthol vapour from his electronic cigarette before re-focussing his thoughts and walking the short distance to Robert Street and home.

***

He slipped off his shoes before wiping them and inserting wooden shoetrees, a habit. Even now, when he was secure inside, the room seemed cold and a little depressing; the only welcome was the intermittent red flash from the answer phone light signalling his attention. Some people had animals to welcome their return, all wagging tails and barks but for Cyril it was always the blinking Cyclopic eye of the phone. He had messages but as it was Sunday, they would wait. He tossed the catalogue onto the coffee table. He needed a beer.

***

The black, plastic cable-tie bit into her tender flesh as Valerie, in a desperate attempt to work free, twisted her arms that were secured above her head and around what she believed to be the rough, low branch of a tree. She had been left to stand uncomfortably on the balls of her bare feet. Occasionally she weakened and her captured wrists painfully held her full weight. The tape across her mouth made breathing difficult and that covering her eyes rendered her blind.

At times, when the wind blew with more force, rain stung her exposed, sensitive flesh, the weather now seemed to be against her too, the ally of her human tormentor. Colours flashed and floated within the trapped darkness of her eyes as the rainwater dripped from her hair. It ran down her face, mixing a cocktail of sadness as it blended with her leaking tears. All she could do was ask herself, "Why?" She had been a little late, yes and taken a short cut she might not have walked under normal circumstances, but then the circumstances were anything but normal. She had been desperate, she needed a toilet, it was to take only a minute away from the road. *How did they know I was here? How could they know that I'd just go into the bushes away from the road? Why me? Why this? What have I done?* The questions tumbled into a confused Gordian knot, a maelstrom of fear, panic and uncertainty. Her head felt compressed, confused, dulled... she tried to remember. What could they possibly want?

She thought of Paul, her lover. His face swam illicitly into her mind. He was laughing and holding the bright red pill on his outstretched index finger before quickly retracting it into his enclosed palm like a magician. Why had he dropped her off where he did? Surely her duplicity hadn't been discovered? She forcibly cleared her mind of the thought... she'd been foolish twice. What would her partner, John, make of this? What would she tell him? She began to cry even more.

Her captor moved around the hanging figure, a red glow from a headlamp lightly illuminated the immediate surroundings adding to the macabre scene. The red filter ensured light would not spill from the darkness.

The rain stopped but the wind continued to blow. She felt the damp leaves between her toes and the cold made her shiver with involuntary, jerking movements as if she were dancing to the wind's tune. She knew where she was and she knew whoever held her was close by, watching, waiting. Occasionally, only occasionally, she sensed that he had moved closer; it was then that she felt the warmth of his breath on the side of her cheek. Her sense of smell had grown more acute and she could detect a trace of garlic, just the faintest whiff but it was there. She turned her face towards the breath, strangely finding some bizarre comfort; it was human and it was familiar.

She had tried to kick out once, hoping to strike lucky, but she had immediately felt the retaliation, a sharp pain had flashed through her face as the flat palm of a hand had struck her nose. It had been hard enough to make her panic and see small, bright lights in the darkness. She had been momentarily unable to draw in air, but the calculated blow had been tempered and gentle enough not to block her airway with blood. It was then that she had heard his voice for the first time.

"Bright eyes, that was foolish, how disappointing."

She gasped again. She had heard the voice before and her confused mind tried to put a face to the words. She failed.

Time seemed to hang alongside her. Drips from the high branches hit the ground as if counting the seconds of her torment. The metronomic drone of occasional traffic on wet roads was just audible in the background. Life went on, even at this hour. She felt helpless.

The garlic breath came again, this time close to her ear. The breathing was slow and precise. It wrapped the cold surface of her face with a bizarre security and for one brief moment she thought that she might still be released from this silly game. How wrong she was to grasp such a fine, false hope.

***

Cyril sipped the Black Sheep beer and turned the pages of the catalogue. He was only interested in the art. He glanced up peering over the top of his reading glasses at the Theodore Major oil painting, illuminated by the small spotlight positioned on the wall above the phone. He then noticed the flashing answer phone again. He couldn't leave it any longer, as always, curiosity got the better of him.

"You have two new messages, first message, received today at 10:15." The automated female voice was raw but quickly gave way to familiar, warm tones.

"Cyril, the body is clean but I need to talk ASAP. Miss you."

"Message two received today at 11:22am…"

"Cyril, I've tried your mobile… call me. It's urgent."

"End of messages."

Both were from Julie, Dr Julie Pritchett. He deleted them before dialling her number. He always felt afrisson of excitement as he returned her call. Julie had worked as one of the North East Home Office Pathologists for a number of years and gradually they had developed a relaxed, somewhat uncomplicated but intimate relationship. Neither wished to commit fully and so the occasional date was ideal for both. Everyone knew about it but nothing was said openly. Initially, the gossips at the station referred to it as clinical, convenient, selfish and a few believed it to be unprofessional, but on the whole the majority believed it to be none of their business and after a while nothing was said.

"Good evening, Julie, sorry not to get back to you sooner." He was truly upset that he had not called earlier.

"Cyril, where've you been all day and where's your mobile? They're called mobiles so they stay with you so you can be contacted, not left at home on the kitchen table to keep the cat amused!"

"Haven't got a cat," Cyril protested, his voice flat, playing her along.

"I know… Good God man! I was making a… Never mind. Listen, some of us have been working. The Coulson body, the guy with the missing finger ends, well, we've found them!" There was a pause and Cyril wondered whether she wanted him to make a guess. He was wrong!

"They were in his stomach contents. Whoever did that to him, made him eat them."

Neither spoke as Cyril tried to filter what he had just heard. He had spent a long time in the force and thought he was impervious to what human beings were capable of doing to each other; again he was wrong, twice within two minutes, if he were honest with himself. His skin was not as thick as he had thought it was. He had read somewhere that the epidermis grew thinner with age and maybe the medical researchers were right.

"Do we know how the finger tips were removed?"

"From what we can see, the most likely tool for amputation was tin-snips or secateurs, a slow and painful process. Evidence is clear that the removal was done over a period of a couple of days and from the state of degradation of the fingertips, they were all consumed at the same time. There are also marks on the body to suggest he'd been strapped down. Tests prove the adhesive was from strong tape. Forensics is running comparisons against samples kept to find the manufacturer and I should have that by tomorrow. However, one definite fact is that he died in a kneeling position, submissive, possibly begging before the coup de grâce! Can you get in early tomorrow?" Julie didn't wait for an answer. "What are you doing tonight?"

"Nothing, I'll pick you up." He checked his watch. "Say eight?"

Cyril heard a kiss blown down the phone. "Eight and no shop talk, it'll keep 'til tomorrow." She hung up.

***

The garlic seemed stronger, closer, but now the smell no longer held that sense of comfort. In contradiction, a hand gently cupped the back of Valerie's head holding her face slightly to the right. The faint tinkle of some jewellery rattling seemed familiar, the hand and evocative sound felt reassuring, almost tender. She made herself relax… maybe this joke was finally over. It was then that she felt the pain, searing, hot and intense like none she had felt before; it burned into her right eye socket as the fine steel shaft burst her eyeball. Mucus erupted from her right nostril, as her body twisted and contorted like an outraged marionette; the tape muffled her scream but the escaping sound was loud. Fingers grasped her nose stifling the noise. The blockage of air made her kick and shake until the fingers clamping her nostrils were removed allowing the cold air to flood her lungs.

It would take just one more push from the flat palm onto the elaborately decorated Charles Horner hatpin to send the tip completely through the eye socket and into the frontal lobe of her brain. That movement though, for the moment at least, could wait. There were things that he wanted her to understand fully before that would happen and there was something he wanted to know.

***

Six days earlier.

Colin Coulson had finished his twelve-hour night shift and was hungry as always. Like every other workday, he had chained his bike to the metal cycle stand situated near the top of Cambridge Street, before popping in to the café for a full English breakfast. On this occasion, he had not got as far as the café nor his breakfast.

Cyril reflected on the case as he walked to Julie's flat. Coulson had not turned up for work and there was no sign of disturbance at his apartment. His bike was found where he had left it, apart from a missing front wheel. The café owner seemed surprised that one of his regulars had just stopped turning up and had provided an accurate date and time of his last visit. The CCTV footage from the bus station confirmed that Coulson had arrived on his bicycle before moving off in the direction of the café but there the trail ended. There was nothing else. He had simply disappeared for seventy-two hours before his body was located in Oak Beck down from the Penny-Pot Lane crossing. The corpse had obviously been dumped from a passing vehicle. A thorough search of the surrounding area had found nothing apart from the front wheel of Coulson's bicycle a hundred metres from the naked body. The wheel had proved puzzling as five spokes had been deliberately, yet neatly clipped and removed whilst leaving the rim and tyre in place; Cyril knew it was significant. The police had requested support from the general public and a photograph of the missing man had appeared on the local news, in the press and on social media. Apart from the usual bogus or inaccurate sightings, there had been nothing. It always amazed Cyril that a person could simply disappear and nobody would really care. Only when a body was discovered and police enquiries were made did people wake up to the fact that there might be a problem. Even Coulson's having an exemplary attendance record at work made little difference. Yes, his employer had telephoned his mobile on three occasions but on receiving no answer, nothing further had been done. It had been assumed that he had taken time off!

"It sometimes happens," were his employer's embarrassed words. "When's the funeral?"

Cyril smiled inwardly at the nonchalant swiftness of the insincere question and wondered just how many people truly cared. The cynic in him wondered if Coulson would be missed at all.

The rain was persistent as Cyril made his way, umbrella in hand, up the path that led to Julie's home as he rang the bell. He noticed Julie move the blinds in the bay window of her ground floor apartment. She gave a wave before holding up one finger. Cyril simply pulled a face and shook his head; he'd experienced better welcomes. The door opened and she leaned to kiss him.

"Thanks for coming out. Been a busy day! Italian?" She smiled and kissed him again.

Cyril simply smiled and turned. It would take five minutes to walk to the restaurant. Julie linked his arm and moved closer, taking full advantage of the umbrella.

Chapter Three

As usual, Cyril placed the cup and saucer onto the mat; like his office, his desk was always tidy and orderly. He tucked the security pass that hung round his neck into his shirt breast pocket. He had thirty minutes before his appointment with Julie regarding Colin Coulson's post mortem. A small pile of documents had been dropped in a tray to the left of his computer and a number of Post-it notes of differing colours had been attached to his computer screen. To his annoyance they were placed without structure nor order. One, however, caught his eye for two reasons: firstly, it was upside down and secondly it included the word *FLASH*! He knew who had placed it there and it brought a smile to his lips.

Flash had been Cyril's sobriquet during his early career. Many thought it a reference to his impeccable dress sense and appearance but they were wrong; it was the link with Bennett that had brought the attachment. Originally, he was nicknamed *Gordon* after the philanthropic industrialist with a passion for fast cars and speed, the man who provided the Gordon Bennett Trophy, but then, with the resurrection of the comic character *Flash Gordon,* Cyril became known as *Flash.* It would be a brave subordinate who would use it within earshot today though. He was to be known as Sir, neither Boss nor Chief, it had to be Sir. Owen and Julie seemed to be the only two who dared to sail close to the wind.

'NEWS FLASH!'

Colin Coulson – Please refer to email regarding finds on his computer and phone.

Owen

Sipping his tea, Cyril turned on his computer before noting that he had sixteen emails, fewer than usual, the day was steadily improving. Owen's mail was second from the top.

'*Tech Forensics has trawled through Coulson's IT. It appears that our man is quite a political animal, using social media to voice his political, personal views and prejudices in very strong and somewhat bigoted terms. Very anti drugs from his comments, the plague of the nation! For some of the messages he's collected a number of 'friends' but he's also attracted a considerable number of, shall we say, people who don't share his, seemingly extreme and libellous viewpoints. I have a list of these and those who have un-followed. We should have true names and addresses today. Strangely, he always signed off as* '*Little Piggy*'. *Just wondered if that was the reason he lost his fingers! Symbolic gesture?*'

Cyril glanced at the top file before opening the cover but could not prevent the nursery rhyme from coming immediately to mind. He felt the fingers on his left hand move to the rhyme. The file contained the history of Coulson's communications on social media. As he thumbed through them it was clear that Owen had been right, they were volatile and at times libellous and vindictive. From what Cyril had gleaned about Coulson's character, this side of him was obviously saved for his faceless, Internet anonymity. The phone rang.

"Bennett."

"You're late, Cyril Bennett, by ten minutes!" Dr Julie Pritchett paused. "Not a good start to the week. No point having a bloody expensive watch and then ignoring it."

Cyril glanced at his watch, a Rolex, a fortieth birthday gift to himself. How long ago that seemed.

"Sorry, got carried away with our friend Coulson. Had a strange streak to his character. Owen has a theory that his vindictive Internet communications might explain the reason he was killed and why he lost the ends of his fingers. Without them you can't communicate using a keyboard! This little piggy didn't go all the way home either!"

"Sorry? You're not making sense but it's Monday morning, you're forgiven, Cyril. There's something else regarding his stomach contents apart from his fingers. We've found traces of paper, some of which was only partially digested. It was obviously fed to him in pieces, maybe even wrapped round the fingers like a bun covering a hotdog, nothing would surprise me! The truth is, Cyril, we're not too sure. But it might corroborate Owen's theory too." There was a pause. "Maybe, and this is just thinking out loud after what you said… have they made 'Piggy' eat his own words?"

"What, like pigs in blankets?" Cyril mumbled feeling suddenly nauseous at the possibility.

Julie pulled an involuntary face reflecting her own disgust. "The samples are still being investigated but it's doubtful you'll get much from them. We've also taken some samples from around the tape marks and from what's left of his hands. Toxicology results will take a little time. Are you interested in cause of death?"

Cyril removed his reading glasses and put his hand to his forehead. He had made the assumption, wrongly he was soon to discover, that Coulson had died from the trauma of amputation and blood loss. "Sorry, I thought it was…" He didn't finish.

"We've found evidence of damage to the area at the base of the neck hair line. There's a puncture wound showing entry to the *foramen magnum,* which you know is at the base of the occipital bone. The fine needle has penetrated the whole brain causing major bleeding and death."

"Bicycle spoke?" Cyril asked optimistically and then paused. "Could it be a sharpened bicycle spoke that caused the damage?"

Julie was taken aback by the swiftness of his response. "Whatever it was, Cyril, it was thin and long, I'd say five to seven inches. It left little external bleeding which tells me that it was very fine."

"I'll bring in a spoke and you can see. We've nothing as yet regarding his clothing. Thanks, Julie. And thanks for your company last night."

"Just a pity you didn't want to stay! Had you done so, you wouldn't have missed our morning meeting. I'll send across images of the stomach contents within the next ten minutes. Believe me, you'll never touch a hot dog again." She giggled and hung up.

Cyril shook his head and smiled before sipping more of his tea. It was now cold.

***

Valerie no longer felt pain from her strapped wrists, this having been superseded by the throbbing, searing agony of what seemed to be a series of electrical discharges; that shot down her left side until they reached the tips of her toes, even though the pain was emanating from the right eye socket. She struggled to breathe, her nasal airway now being partially blocked by the flowing stream of thick mucus. She coughed and choked. As if to alleviate the sensation, she tried to turn her head to ease the throbbing by resting it against her shoulder but that proved impossible. She physically curled her body inwards fighting against the pain and the resulting nausea and then, as suddenly as it had arrived, it ceased. There was no gradual fading but a sudden cessation and her body relaxed involuntarily; it had reached its natural endurance of suffering and her body was closing down. Now, she neither felt the cold, nor heard the sound of cars in the distance, it was as if she were closeted away, cocooned and somehow protected. Images now flooded her mind's eye as they swam before her bringing a moment's respite. She neither sensed, nor heard the movements from close by. An invisible hand was raised, its palm flat, inches from the finial at the top of the protruding hatpin.

"You've told me nothing so let's play a little game. I spy with my little..."

That voice! Her mind seemed to clear and she smiled behind the tape that stretched over her mouth. It was a sudden recognition, for at that moment she knew who stood near. Suddenly relieved, she turned in the direction from where the voice had come.

The palm struck hard, driving the pin backwards and upwards into the frontal lobe of her brain. Valerie's legs kicked spasmodically and her toes buried themselves into the soft, leaf-layered earth as if grasping for false hope. A trickle of urine flushed down her inner thighs pooling round her blackened feet. The voice came again as she was saying the final word to herself.

"... Eye."

She also called out a name but the tight gag muffled the sound.

As she was dying, she heard the sound of the traffic and somewhere close by, an owl called as a familiar face drifted into her consciousness and then... there was nothing.

Her clothing was swiftly removed, cut and torn away. A hand was raised holding a blade. It cut through the strong, plastic electrical tie that bit into Valerie's warm but dead flesh. The now-naked body crumpled to the ground forming a grotesque, unnatural shape on the wet mud. The hatpin was slowly withdrawn having been driven even further into the socket, slitting the tape that wrapped her eyes as she had crashed to the ground. Eyes scanned the scene to ensure that nothing had been left. The headlight was turned off and the figure moved away, wrapped within the protective darkness of the parkland.

Chapter Four

Both telephone calls had been received within the space of ten minutes, the first, an emergency call at 06:44, the second was received as a 101 enquiry. Both were about the same person, Valerie Atkins.

Cyril's phone rang and he answered with his usual, "Bennett." He listened and then stood before replacing the receiver. Moving from his office he called out for Owen. David Owen's huge frame appeared, mug in hand, from the kitchen area. He pointed to the mug.

"New. A pressie from the Harrogate International Festival." He smiled proudly.

Cyril read the words printed around the mug. The two that were prominent were *Harrogate* and *Crime.*

"Appropriate, Owen, appropriate."

Owen grinned and took a sip of tea.

"That is, Owen, apart from the word... *Books*!"

Owen lifted and turned the mug to find the word. The twisting manoeuvre allowed some of the contents to dribble down the front of his trousers before hitting his shoes and then the carpet. Cyril just shook his head.

"You've no time for a brew or to dry those. Grab your coat, besides you're supposed to drink it not shower in it!"

Owen looked down at his trousers before brushing them with his hand, allowing more tea to splash over his shoes. He then looked at Cyril. He took one sip before placing the drink onto his desk. Cyril watched as he cleaned his shoes on the backs of his trousers. Owen's body language and facial expression invited the question.

"Jogger's discovered a body at the very far end of Valley Gardens near the junction of Harlow Moor Drive and Harlow Moor Road. The area's been sealed and Scene of Crime are on their way. We've also received a missing person enquiry, female, Ms Valerie Atkins, 28. Her partner called, in worried that she hadn't returned home after a party with her girl friends."

"Two and two makes?" Owen pulled a face. "Could be one and the same but then again. Body… male or female?"

"Female."

"Makes four," chipped in Owen swiftly.

Cyril and Owen had worked together for a number of years; they were opposites, poles apart, as different as chalk is from cheese, but they were a strong team, each complementing the other. For Cyril, Owen was an amicable colleague, totally reliable and trustworthy and formidable in a crisis. His height and stature made him an intimidating force when required. To Owen, a spade was a spade it was that simple. He was the grit that formed the pearl of their professional relationship.

Owen drove. He listened to Cyril as he waited for the barrier to lift to allow them to exit the secure parking area of the new Harrogate station. Leaves fell as strong gusts flailed the trees separating the police station from the road. Once at the station entrance, they turned right onto Beckwith Head Road and then right down Otley Road. The morning sky was still a dismal grey but there was an optimistic glow like raw, chapped skin that cracked along the skyline as they headed east. The crime scene was three minutes away. On turning down Harlow Moor Road, Cyril glanced across at St Andrew's, the Police Treatment Centre. He smiled to himself, secure in the knowledge that with all the pressures the job forced upon his colleagues, there were always professional people there to help put mind and body back together.

Owen slowed and turned on the blue strobe lights that ran brightly within the car's grille. The officer controlling traffic had already recognised the car and pointed to a spot on the pavement just before a mini roundabout. Owen parked as directed.

A number of police vehicles were already haphazardly parked before the blue and white police tape that had been strung from a street sign to a tree, closing Harlow Moor Drive to the public.

"Busy!" Owen put on his coat followed by a police fluorescent over-jacket as they made their way to the tape.

Cyril signed the log held by an officer standing on the periphery of the tape before they entered the crime scene area. It was 07:41.

A dog handler appeared briefly from the heavily wooded park border before disappearing into the undergrowth further down the road. Without warning the heaven's opened and the rain swept across the scene. White-suited Forensic Officers moved, alien-like, between their vehicles and the trees, seemingly oblivious to the weather.

"We've a female, cause of death unknown at present. Doctor Caner is on site." Caner was one of three North East Home Office Pathologists. Cyril had been expecting it to be Julie.

"Access is through there."

A finger pointed to a gap in the trees marked by red tape as coverall, overshoes and gloves were handed to Cyril.

"Only one person if you don't mind, Sir."

The smile was forced. "Not much room if you get my drift."

Cyril looked at Owen as he stepped into the oversized suit. He then squeezed past two of the Forensic team as he entered the wooded area. Within a minute he came upon another plastic cordon. Illuminated by strong LED lights, Cyril noted the many coloured, numbered markers that were dotted around the outside of the white tent that was tightly positioned between trees, sheltering the crime scene from the weather and potential onlookers. He waited, checking his watch before shaking his wrist and looking again. It was now 08:04. Dr Caner left the tent, saw Cyril and raised a gloved hand.

"Drawn the short straw, Cyril?" Caner smiled before ducking under the tape, his coverall hood still over his head and the mask now hanging around his throat.

"Intriguing." He nodded to the tent. "Female, probably died bound to that tree branch. Appears to have been suspended by her wrists." His blue-gloved finger pointed to the tree to the left of the tent.

Cyril's eyes followed in the direction indicated. He noticed the marks where the bark had been discoloured through the rubbing and a numbered marker was pinned to the left of the abrasions. Below was a further collection of erect, plastic numbers. Cyril recognised Hannah Peters, Dr Julie Pritchett's assistant, photographing what seemed to be indiscernible. She looked across and nodded.

Caner continued. "I should say it's my belief at this early stage, that the spot chosen was no accident. I believe that the victim was brought here, let's say that it was convenient. From my assessment, that branch was a perfect height, but we should leave that to these people. Time of death approximately two to three hours ago but not definitive as you know," Cyril smiled and raised his eyebrows. "I'll have a clearer picture later."

"Cause of death?" Cyril sucked on his electronic cigarette but inhaled no vapour. He looked at it realising that the battery had also given up the ghost. He returned it to his pocket.

"Now here's the funny thing. Although the corpse is naked, the clothing was removed post mortem. I'm fairly certain of that. I also believe that she was stabbed through the right eye, the weapon or blade penetrating the brain. Judging by the tape covering the eyes, the entry wound indicates that the weapon was very narrow and very long. Apart from marks where she was bound and strung up by the wrists, there's no further tissue damage. Maybe sexual but no genital trauma noted here but we'll see when we perform the full examination. Clinical and somewhat calculated if you ask me." The doctor paused, noting Cyril's inquisitive expression. "Look Cyril, as I've said, once we have her back and the autopsy is done, I'll have some facts for you but that's all I can say for now. You'll be attending I take it?"

Caner did not wait for a response but politely pushed past, his bag lifted to his chest to prevent it from touching the trunks of the young trees that seemed to be everywhere.

The Scene of Crimes' Manager walked towards Cyril and handed him an iPad. Cyril removed a glove before flicking through the images that were on screen. Occasionally he turned his head to judge the perspective before spreading his fingers to enlarge a certain element of the image.

"They're with you now but thought you'd like to take a quick shufty. No sign of clothing or a weapon. We're taking a number of imprints, the ground is fairly rich in those. We'll do a fingertip search once we've cleared here. The park's been sealed."

Cyril followed the route back. Owen was leaning against a van as he emerged from the woodland, chatting to one of the Forensic team. The rain had stopped for the time being. Owen noticed Cyril emerge, smiled and tapped the female Scene of Crime Officer on the shoulder. She turned and followed Owen's stare, the conversation was over.

"Miserable bugger, Caner," observed Owen. "Didn't take me on apart from a perfunctory nod. Always looks like he's lost a tanner and found a penny… mind working with the dead on a daily basis must affect you at sometime." He found no response in Cyril's facial expression. "I've called through for someone to get a photograph of the missing woman to compare with that of the body. It'll be back at the station on our return."

Owen smiled and winked at the CSI to whom he had been talking as she turned to leave.

"Friendly chat, Owen, or business?" Cyril tried again to retrieve some menthol vapour from his e-cigarette as he spoke but was unsuccessful. "I suggest you keep your professional opinions on Caner to yourself when in the company of, let's say, other colleagues." Cyril turned and looked at the white-suited figure walking back to the trees. "Careless talk, Owen! Careless talk! I take it you've been too busy to organise door to door along Harlow Moor Lane and Drive and the roads backing on?"

"Not standing idle whilst you head off into the wilderness and the unknown, Sir." He smiled, trying to regain his equilibrium after receiving Cyril's pointed criticism. "They're starting here shortly, closest to the scene. Also called in for news coverage to be ready for social media and the local press."

Cyril simply smiled. *Keen,* he thought, before heading for the car. *Sometimes misguided but keen as mustard.*

The officer who was ordering the traffic moved towards Cyril.

"The lady over there lives in this house and witnessed something last night. I've asked her to wait to have a word, Sir."

"Excellent, well done! What's her name?"

"Miss Allen, Dorothy Allen."

Cyril smiled and put a hand on the PSCO's shoulder before moving off towards her. "Thank you!"

"Miss Allen? DCI Cyril Bennett and this is DS Owen. Thank you for waiting. I believe you saw something that might be of interest?"

"Has someone died?" She didn't wait for a reply. "I sleep in that room there, live in the upper apartment." She turned and pointed to a second floor square-cornered bay window. "Last night I couldn't sleep and sat in the bay. I could see the streetlights further down the road were on but the light opposite wasn't working. Strange, really, as they've only recently been installed with those bright LED ones, but for some reason this one opposite is a reluctant light!"

She paused and smiled. Cyril wondered if that was all that she had to tell him but then she took a deep breath.

"At two thirty I saw someone get out of a car at the top of the road, a woman I'm sure. She waited for the car to leave and then she quickly came down the road; seemed to be a bit unsteady on her pins." She noticed Cyril's reaction to the word. "Pins, her legs, Inspector."

Cyril nodded his understanding and smiled.

"Just opposite here she stopped and looked around as if she were checking to see if there was anyone about. She looked up but because of the net curtains and no bedroom light I don't think she saw me. She then nipped into the bushes and trees. I assumed she was going for a pee. A night out, drink and then feeling the cold we've all been there." She smiled and looked at both officers for reassurance.

Owen nodded. "A bit tricky for a lady."

Dorothy seemed to relax. "It was then that I noticed another person moving across the road; I thought it was a man this time. He entered the tree line just higher up. I have to admit it made me smile. Here I was thinking she was answering a call of nature when all along she was answering a much stronger call. Don't see much of that at this time of year. In spring and summer you'd be amazed at what goes on in those trees and bushes." She raised her eyebrows and tutted. "Disgusting some of the things I'd say."

"What happened then?"

Cyril turned and looked at the line of foliage and trees running to the left of the road.

"Nothing, neither reappeared. Besides, I checked my bedside clock and it was two-fifty eight so I went back to bed. The next thing I heard was your people outside. I took something to help me sleep."

"Can you show me exactly where they both entered the trees?"

She smiled and nodded before walking across the road.

"He entered here and she…" She walked five or six paces to the tape before pointing. "… there."

Cyril turned to Owen. "Find the Crime Scene Manager and mention that they need to broaden the area. Point out the two specific entrances identified and get it sealed off. Thank you, Miss Allen. Here's my number. If anything else comes to mind then please call me anytime. We'll need to speak with you again but I'm grateful for your help this morning." Cyril held out his hand and shook hers.

She smiled and walked back across the street, occasionally looking at the card she had received before turning back on reaching the pavement.

"Inspector! One thing. After a few minutes there was what I can only describe as an occasional red glow that came and went in the trees about there." She pointed and waved her hand giving a vague direction. "I've never heard of professional girls taking their welcome sign with them, have you?"

Cyril simply smiled and thanked her again, immediately realising that a red light would allow vision in the dark whilst maintaining good night vision once the light was switched off. He now knew that after what Caner had suspected and the information about the red light, that the murder was most definitely planned.

Owen returned. The police tape was then adjusted to close off the upper entry point.

"That was lucky, Sir. Might have missed some vital evidence. Nice lady! Strong breath though… must have enjoyed an evening curry!"

Cyril looked at Owen. "Didn't notice, Owen."

Owen just raised his shoulders before returning to the car. He removed the fluorescent jacket and tossed it into the back seat. Cyril's phone announced he had mail. He checked. An image of the missing woman appeared.

"We have a match, Owen. It's Valerie Atkins's body.

He slipped the phone into his pocket and climbed in. "There's a connection, Owen. Our friend here was murdered with a fine object inserted into the brain through the right eye. Coulson died in a similar manner; one entry from the front, the other from the rear. I doubt we have a coincidence. Who did this might be one and the same."

He removed his dead e-cigarette and simply sucked on it. Owen looked across and smiled inwardly before starting the car.

Chapter Five

"It's either a fine surgical implement, some type of needle or a long pin that's been used in both murders." Julie stood looking at the head-scan images taken from both brains; to Cyril they were but two similar coloured, intricate yet beautiful patterns.

"Both implements have the same diameter and although it may not be the same instrument that was used to commit both murders, the dimensions and length appear to be very similar. It's conjecture at this stage, the depth of penetration will be determined by either the weapon's length or the force applied. Neither appears to have hit bone, only penetrated the soft tissue. We've located some fine, oxidised residue from the adhesive tape that covered the eye. When the implement was extracted, minute surface elements adhered to the sticky perforation within the tape. So, it's not stainless steel or a modern surgical material."

"Bicycle spoke?" Cyril offered tentatively again, but seeing Julie's immediate shaking of the head, he did not pursue it.

"Early medical implement or long pin, industrial or… the steel used in ladies' hatpins. After all, ladies of the Social and Political Union, Suffragettes to you and me, Cyril, were ordered to remove their hatpins whilst in court. You can understand when you see the length of these potential weapons."

Cyril burned inside. He hated being lectured to on the bleeding obvious, and particularly on subjects of which he felt he had a degree of understanding. He knew just who the SPU were. To make his point he responded by informing Julie that cities like Berlin and New York had banned the wearing of such 'weapons' in the early part of the twentieth century. Sadly, it did not make him feel any better, it just sounded foolishly pompous. He looked away.

Julie blushed slightly realising that she had touched a raw nerve. "As you rightly say, Cyril, a hatpin would make a perfect weapon."

Cyril looked at the scans one more time and as his embarrassment subsided, he simply smiled and winked.

"Charles Horner, the famous Victorian Yorkshire hatpin designer and maker. Some of his pieces are wonderfully elaborate. Come up for auction regularly. Not silly money either. Did you know he was from Halifax?"

Julie got the message. "Can't see you as a pin collector, Cyril, but then who knows what you keep concealed in your secret places?" She winked back.

Cyril chuckled. "Just trying to impress a beautiful lady." He turned to leave.

"Job done then. Call me!" She saw him nod as he raised his hand.

***

After studying the photographs taken at the crime scene, Owen read through the notes on his laptop.

Valerie Atkins, 28.
Freelance Broadcast Journalist. Leeds Trinity University, degree in journalism, Post degree attachment to Sky (Five months) and BBC (Two months) before working freelance. Success with her first documentary, 'Blame Makes the Claim.'
Partner, John Cooper, primary school teacher, lived together for two years (On and off). Address…

As he read on Owen twisted and gnawed at the heavily-chewed pencil that protruded from his lips and pondered the meaning of "on and off". Somehow he knew that his interpretation was definitely rude and way off target! He still chuckled to himself like a mischievous schoolboy before making a note to question the nature of their relationship when they interviewed Cooper. He continued to study the notes, jotting down relevant addresses and dates.

Cyril quietly moved to stand behind him and glanced down at the notes. "Take Liz..."

Owen dropped the pencil as Cyril spoke. "Jesus Christ, Sir! You're like bloody smoke, made me jump!" Owen stuttered, startled that Cyril had positioned himself so closely without his knowledge.

"Vapour, Owen, simply vapour, definitely not smoke." He inhaled his e-cigarette. "Take Liz and interview Valerie Atkins's parents. A Community Support Officer has been there and reports that they're holding up quite well. Usual stuff; get them to show you her room. If the relationship with Copper is as has been reported, let's say a little capricious, she'll still have a bed there. Jumpy today Owen or is it guilt?"

"What about John Cooper, shouldn't we be..."

Cyril raised a finger. "It's in hand." He smiled and moved away followed by a thin cloud of minty vapour. "Still thinking of the lady in white?"

Owen laughed. "Very good, Sir," as he heard Cyril whistle the tune to *Lady in Red*. He reached for the phone. "I see what you did there, Sir, funny."

"Liz? Get your coat, I'll brief you on the way."

Liz Graydon had been transferred from Leeds as a promoted Detective Sergeant just over eighteen months ago. Although seemingly inept initially, her determined professional attitude, her toughness mixed with a generous helping of sensitivity, made her adapt quickly within the team. She had a soft spot for Owen. Even though she was a year or two his junior, she would often mother him, straighten his tie, adjust his collar or be a receptive pair of ears. Cyril would often smile on seeing them together, Liz's wisp-like frame contrasting with the height and bulk of Owen but he had immediately seen their potential; they were now a strong pairing.

***

Mrs Atkins was younger than Owen had imagined. She was petite, blonde with startling blue eyes. The only tell tale signs that she had suffered tragedy were the deepening dark rings that shadowed her lower eyelids.

"Mrs Atkins?"

She smiled.

"DS Owen and this is DS Graydon. May we have a word? Is your husband in?"

She glanced at the proffered warrant card and opened the door fully before turning and walking into the first room on the left of the hall. Liz followed first and offered her condolences. There was a candle lit in a small tea-light holder next to a photograph of Valerie, reflecting the solemnity.

Liz returned her gaze to Valerie's mother. "When was the last time you saw your daughter?" Liz's voice was direct but sensitive.

"I think it was Friday, yes Friday last week. She popped in to tell us that a television company had accepted an important project she'd been working on. She was a bundle of happiness and nerves. I can't remember the last time she was so bubbly. She couldn't rest. I opened some wine and we had a small celebration. If only it had been Champagne!"

She seemed to drift off back to the moment, reliving the security of that last happy meeting. Owen looked at Liz and she raised a hand from her knee as if to signal that he should just give her a little time.

"Sorry, just got carried away… who was it that said memories are cushions for later life?" A small smile contradicted the tear that ran down her cheek. "I'll be able to sit comfortably won't I, I've so many."

"What project was that?" Owen asked as he glanced at the number of framed photographs that stood on the side table. He recognised those of Valerie behind the candle.

"Project?"

"The television company."

"Sorry, yes, forgive me. She never said. Never talked about work other than if she'd been accepted or rejected, Sergeant. She would keep her work to herself. I can say there were far more rejections though. It was so sad. Our daughter was very focussed, even when she was a little girl. She'd spend hours in her room reading or with her homework. She was diligent. We've been lucky really…" She paused and collected herself. More tears began to run down her cheeks. "Sorry, for a moment the reality of the situation had escaped me. Why would someone want to harm our Valerie, she was so innocent!"

Owen noted her words. '*… for a moment the reality of the situation had escaped me.*' It sounded so strange, as if rehearsed.

"Is your husband at home? Maybe we could speak with him."

"No, he's shopping. Life goes on as they say and we have to eat although to be honest I have little appetite for food or for life at the moment. It will pass, when though, I'm not too sure as yet, but it must. We did overcome evil in the past when tragedy struck and we shall again. We have a strong faith."

"What about her siblings?"

"James and Jennifer, I think you know Jennifer died in a road accident when she was seven, drunk driver they told us, never caught. James teaches in Wigan, a primary school in a place called Hindley Green. We've never been. Never invited. But it sounds lovely. That's how Valerie met John, he and James were colleagues when they first started teaching. James moved to Wigan for promotion two years ago. Rarely see him, even considering the consequences. He's phoned, of course, to ask when the funeral is but that's all. Ever since the death of his younger sister his personality changed. He seemed to erect an emotional force field around himself. He's cold, a bit like his dad."

Liz quickly glanced at Owen. "May we see Valerie's room?"

Mrs Atkins dabbed her eyes with the small handkerchief before tucking it up the sleeve of her sweater. "I'll put the kettle on whilst you do whatever police people do. Milk and sugar?"

"In tea? One, milk and two sugars, one just milk. Thanks."

The bedroom was small, tidy and definitely feminine. Both slipped on gloves. Owen picked up the only framed photograph in the room and he assumed it to be Valerie's dead sister, Jennifer. Liz went through the wardrobe and then the drawers. There was a selection of clothing for most occasions.

"Still feels as though she needs a second base or bolt hole. Kind of suggests the relationship had its shaky times."

Liz went to the white tall-boy. Starting at the top drawer, she swept her hand to the back of the drawer checked the contents and then did the same to the next one down. The bottom drawer she slid and lifted out completely. On the base of the tall-boy was a black metal box, an odd sock, a pair of knickers that had fallen from one of the drawers and a copious amount of fluff and dust. Liz tried to lift the lid of the box without success. She noted Owen's surprise and pre-empted his question.

"Every little girl has her secret place. Love letters and the like," she smiled. "Don't little boys?"

Owen just pulled a face before shaking his head. "Would never remember where I'd put the stuff. Tended to dump everything on the floor. My mother used to go mad!"

"Tea's ready!" Mrs Atkins popped her face round the door, her eyes immediately falling on the box. "What's that?"

"It was at the bottom of this chest of drawers. I'd like to take it to the station to go through it. Do you have the key?"

"I've never seen it before. To be honest, I rarely came in here. Val did all her own cleaning. Once she turned seventeen, she requested that her privacy be respected. I understood that." She pointed to the key in the door. "This is the spare. It's normally always locked."

"The contents will be itemised. We'll need another twenty-minutes in here but I'm ready for a cuppa."

Liz stood and moved to the door after placing the box on the bed. Owen never took his eyes from Mrs Atkins's face. He could sense the fascination the box held for her but then he realised that she was aware that she was being scrutinised. She turned to leave the room.

On their return, Owen checked under the bed and Liz went through the pockets of each item of clothing hanging in the wardrobe. There was nothing, nothing of interest, that is, apart from the box.

Liz wrote out a receipt for the box and handed it to Mrs Atkins.

"We'll return everything once the investigation is completed."

Owen finalised his notes with a list of Valerie's friends and colleagues before they left.

"Just one more thing, Mrs Atkins," Owen always felt like the old TV detective Columbo when he asked a question upon leaving. He almost wanted to partly close one eye and suck his pencil for the full effect. "Did she have a computer in the house?"

"She always uses a laptop and one of those electronic pads, always carries them with her or uses the phone. Never seems to be off the thing like most young people these days. Neither Fred nor I has a computer at home, sorry. Call us old fashioned."

Owen was surprised considering her age. "What about at work?"

"Needs must when the devil drives, Sergeant."

"So the answer to my question, Mrs Atkins, is?

"Yes, we both use one at work and at work is where they stay."

Owen lifted his head and nodded lightly as if to display acceptance of the answer, which he did, but just, only just.

Once in the car Liz pulled on her seat belt.

"What was all that about? What does it matter if they have a computer at work or not? We're not investigating them we're looking into the horrific death of their daughter."

Owen simply looked at Liz before mumbling, "We'll see!"

***

Cyril stared at the images on screen taken of Colin Coulson's stomach contents. He used the remote to zoom in on the pictures taken of the paper fragments but there was nothing he could determine of relevance. He then brought up the Internet and viewed Harrogate on Google Maps, highlighting the image until it focussed on the crime scene area of Valerie Atkins's murder. He pondered the possible routes taken by the murderer. It was amazing just how much of the area was covered by the trees; the pathway linking Harlow Moor Road and the bowling green and then the tennis courts in Valley Gardens was just visible. At the time the murder has been committed, the routes available to leave the scene were numerous. The two dog teams had found nothing, making it more than likely that the murderer had left the woodland as close to the scene as possible and made his escape by car. He made a note to that effect but concluded, 'OR HER' underlining it twice.

DC Stuart Park entered holding a file and dropped it on the desk next to Cyril.

"Door to door? Nothing! Fingertip search carried out up to the clearing in the park..." He pointed to the file. "Plenty, but it's felt nothing relevant to the case. Certain items are with Forensics. You'd be amazed at the stuff that's been trawled."

Cyril simply lifted his eyebrows and smiled a knowing smile.

"There's nothing that could surprise me, Stuart, nothing!" He glanced at the clock on the wall. His phone rang.

"Ruth... sorry! Yes. No, I'm coming. Got carried away here. Just give me five minutes. Sorry!"

"Damn, that's the second appointment time that I've missed; I should be with John Cooper, partner of the deceased to break some bad news. I also want him to identify formally the body but we'll see after I've had a word."

"I take it from your call that Ruth's liaising?" Stuart enquired as he read the information on the boards.

" Yes, Ruth Jones has been attached to parents and partner."

Stuart didn't turn round. "Good luck to her, shit job!"

***

Cyril followed the car belonging to Ruth Jones, the Police Family Liaison Officer as they left the station. She turned off Jenny Fields Drive onto Columbus Close, slowed and stopped in front of number sixteen, a small semi-detached property. The rain had stopped but the day was grey and dull, a fitting tribute to the job in hand. A blue Mini Cooper was parked in the drive. Cyril walked up to Ruth's car.

"Even the car's called Cooper but you can't get attached to that!" Cyril turned and smiled at Ruth, trying to lighten the mood for the grim part of policing that was to follow.

The front door opened before Cyril and Ruth had reached the path and John Cooper filled the frame. He had the appearance of a rugby scrum front row.

"DCI Bennett. Mr Cooper?" He held out his warrant card.

Cooper went to shake it but then saw the proffered item and blushed slightly.

"Any news Inspector?"

"Let me introduce you to your Police Liaison Officer, Ruth Jones, she's attached to the CID and will keep you informed throughout the investig..." He didn't finish.

"It's bad news, I know it is. I heard nothing from the police after the call but then I get the shattering news from Valerie's mother and then you two pop round. What the bloody hell's going on?"

He seemed to move away from them as if they were harbingers of some unseen evil.

Cyril realised that the timing had been terrible and could see a complaint winging its way to the top office. He now knew that there was only one way to deal with this. He knew that it might be cruel and a little inaccurate but… "We'd have brought you out of work earlier today but we had to be sure that the body was Valerie's. I'm sorry to tell you, as I realise you're aware, that we've now identified the body to be Valerie's. A post mortem is being carried out to identify the cause of death. Would you like to sit down?"

Cooper took hold of a chair arm and lowered his bulk.

"We're aware that this comes, even second hand, as a dreadful shock but we believe Valerie was murdered, Mr Cooper." He waited for the information to sink in. Both Ruth and Cyril watched.

"Where… where is she?" A globule of saliva dribbled from the corner of his mouth as he fought to hold back tears.

"She's being looked after. As it's a murder enquiry it's important that I find out as much as possible about her whereabouts last night. It's crucial that we work quickly. Are you up to helping me with answering some questions?"

There was a pause before he nodded.

"Where did Valerie go last night?"

"It'd been planned for a while, some ex University mates had come up to Harrogate for a get together, they do it every now and again. The last meeting was in Leeds."

"Names? Do you have names?"

He nodded again. "A couple that she's always phoning or texting. Gail, Sheila, sorry three there's Nancy too. It's usually a meal and then a bar and if possible a club so the finish time is usually late or early! But with it being a Sunday I assumed she'd be back just after midnight."

Ruth added the names to the notes. "Surnames would be a great help."

"They'll come to me but they're in the address book."

"Strange night to go out late."

"They were out Saturday too. Val slept most of Sunday. It's a full-on weekend bash, not for the faint-hearted. They work hard and believe me, they play hard." He pulled a strange face that meant nothing to Cyril.

"What time did she leave to go out on Sunday?"

"About six thirty. I dropped her off on Albert Street. They were meeting at Pizza Express."

"Were they eating there?"

"Who knows!"

"Did you try to ring her during the evening?"

"No, she rang here about eleven and said she'd be home no later than one, that I should go to bed and not wait up, she'd get a taxi home. To be honest she sounded totally sober."

"Did she say where she was at that time?"

He shook his head. "No, but it was lively, sounded more like a house party than a pub or club. I asked where she was but she just told me to stop fussing."

"You rang 101 at…"

"About six thirty. I woke and found she wasn't here. I checked the house and rang her mobile but nothing. I was shitting myself to be honest." He put his hand to his mouth as if in chastisement. "Sorry, Mrs Jones."

Ruth looked up and smiled. "Please, call me Ruth."

"Sorry, Ruth. I rang her mum to see if she'd gone there but she hadn't. Strangely, I checked the car and even the bath… but…" He put his head in his hands. "I should have stayed up. I could've gone out looking."

"John, Harrogate's a big place. Besides had she wanted you to collect her she'd have telephoned, yes? So, were you here all night apart from the drop off?"

"Yes, marking and preparation for the week ahead. Never stops! This so called 9 til 3:30 job doesn't exist in education, believe me!"

Cyril knew all too well about unpaid overtime. "Do you have the names and addresses?"

"No addresses, only names and telephone numbers, they're by the phone in the hall."

Cyril followed. "Ruth will stay a little longer and go over a few things with you. Contact her whenever and she'll be our link."

John moved a piece of thin metal from the top of an address book.

"What's that?" Cyril enquired.

"God knows! Someone pushed it through the door either late Friday or early Saturday, probably kids."

Cyril moved over to take a closer look. He removed a rubber glove from his pocket and put it on before picking up the thin rod. "It looks like a bicycle spoke. I'll need to take it. Was there anything with it?"

"Val found it, she didn't say. She asked if it was mine. She popped it there meaning to get rid of it I suppose."

Cyril turned the glove inside out trapping the metal spoke inside.

"Again, Mr Cooper, my sincere condolences for your loss and sorry for your not hearing first hand from us. It's been a bit fraught."

Cooper simply smiled and held up a hand. "I had a really bad feeling Chief Inspector Bennett."

At this point the floodgates opened and he leaned against the wall. Ruth came in and led him back to the chair waving for Cyril to leave.

There was still a major question circulating in Cyril's brain as he left the house, a question concerning their relationship and his partner's need to maintain a bolt hole. Something told him that now was neither the time nor the place. What he did have was a major clue. He presumed that the spoke was one of the five missing from the wheel found near Coulson's body and Forensics would quickly establish that. But why would someone send a bicycle spoke to the home of another victim? What was with it, if anything?

Chapter Six

The morning briefing was anything but brief; each person stared at a series of images displayed on the large screen at the far end of the room. Liz stood to the left of it.

"These are images of the secure box we discovered at the bottom of a chest of drawers in Valerie's room. There was no key so we assume Valerie carried it with her or concealed it elsewhere." She flicked the corner of the screen and the image changed. "The contents are as pictured here. There seemed to be no specific order other than the way the written notes were stored. Copies of the notes are in the files you have in front of you. They were secured with a paper clip. You all, apart from Owen, will know what item two is." She referred to a small, pink dildo.

Owen simply pulled a face as the others chuckled. He raised his hand.

"Owen?" Liz pointed to Owen.

"Miss Wurswick, it's a lady's little helper." He sucked the end of his pencil.

There was more laughter.

Liz just shook her head not wanting to encourage him but blushed knowing that she had started the light-hearted diversion.

Order was quickly resumed as Cyril tapped his electronic cigarette on the table. "Can we get on?" He was neither in the mood for jokes nor banal comments.

"Sorry, Sir. It also contained a small packet of tablets, six in all, which are now with forensic toxicology, a packet of three condoms, a swimming medal and an engagement ring. It's worth stating at this stage that she has not been engaged to John Cooper at any time and as far as her parents are concerned she has never been formally engaged; the mother has never seen it before. There was a packet of marijuana, some Rizla rolling papers and another key. We've no idea what that was for. Lastly, the most sensitive of items… there was a memory stick."

Liz held the stick, the only material object evident from the cache. She inserted it into the side of the screen and an icon appeared. She clicked on that and four folder icons emerged. Each was numbered. She clicked on the first and QuickTime player appeared with a still image showing just a table. Liz clicked on the start triangle.

Everyone in the room seemed to lean either towards or away from the screen at the same time as the image became discernible and as they became suddenly aware of what they were viewing. The volume seemed loud and filled the room accompanying the images on screen. The deep breathing increased to accompany the ethereal moans and animalistic grunts; the sounds grew louder as the firm buttocks pounded frantically against the soft flesh of the folded female, enthusiastically bent and stretched over the wooden table. She wore nothing apart from a Venetian mask, decorated with curled playing cards forming a crown and an elaborate collar, the gilded lips preserved in a permanent smile. Her long fingers curled and grasped at the far edge of the tabletop, her back slightly arched to allow maximum penetration. Oil or perspiration glistened along the length of her body, reflecting the bright lights above. Suddenly the thrusting stopped. A hand leaned forward and grasped her neck before pulling her upright to her feet. Quickly, strong hands dropped to her shoulders before urgently guiding her body round whilst at the same time pushing her down to her knees. One hand went swiftly to remove the mask and obediently she opened her mouth. A hand lowered and five blue tablets were placed on the protruding tongue before the image disappeared from screen.

"Each video shows the same female but the male participants are different on each occasion. The masks too change with each recording."

"I assume that the female is Valerie?"Cyril asked. "And the tablets look like Valium." He turned to look at Owen. "Now those are a lady's little helpers, if they are proven to be!"

Owen simply stared back with the puzzled expression a child pulls when asked a mental arithmetic question.

"Pathologist has identified certain consistent body marks to conclude that the female is one and the same. They've also suggested that the tablets are NTZs, a form of black market Valium."

"Obviously Valerie isn't the dedicated, good girl her mother believes she was. A daughter wanting her total privacy at seventeen suggested something strange," Owen grumbled. He looked around and held up the file. "It's in our report."

"What about the notes you mentioned; was their content significant?" Cyril spoke quickly in a desperate attempt to move things on. He never felt comfortable viewing what could only be described as pornography even though it was case-related In his time in the force it certainly was not the first and he knew it would not be the last he would see.

Liz removed the memory stick. "The others are all available on the IT case files and I suggest you look to see if there's anything relevant. They're being studied to see if there are any visual or audible give aways."

She then brought up the image taken of the notes.

"They appear to be love notes. Each makes reference to a day and times but no specific dates. Note they're all torn into a similar heart-shape. The last note…" she brought it up on screen, "it's item 1f' in your pack."

Sexy Sunday.
Rod like steel just thinking about you.
Any time from 24 – usual.
I've sweeties too for a good little girl!
X

"The other notes are similar, as you can see. All four make reference to a time or place. Each mentions a treat or some sort of surprise."

"That's the only one referring to a steel rod, yes?" Stuart questioned.

"Yep!"

"We have a rod of steel that was delivered to her house, we have a rod of steel that was inserted into her right eye. We now have four rods of steel still missing. Forensics confirmed that the spoke delivered to Valerie at Cooper's house was one taken from the bicycle wheel found near Coulson's body."

"What about the papers?" someone asked from the far side of the room.

"Prints belonging to Valerie, otherwise clean but the ICP-MS tests show that there's a strong possibility that they all came from the same sheet of paper, a standard office paper, but because of the variance of the findings that fact cannot be used as evidence but it gives us a reference should we find other paper documentation. However, we're sure they're from one and the same place and probably the same person."

Cyril sighed loudly. "Handwriting?"

"Same hand. Right handed when writing. Inks different apart from the first and second note."

"Lady's little helper?" Cyril asked whilst he frowned at Owen.

"Clean apart from finger prints. DNA is Valerie's. The key's been identified as belonging to an Abus Titalium padlock. We're looking at local distributors..."

Owen interrupted. "The tape's been tracked to one produced for the major DIY store, B&Q so check if they stock that make of lock. Stuart put someone onto that." Stuart made notes and nodded.

Cyril glanced round the room. "It's obvious from the personal items found that there was more to Valerie than meets the eye. There's drug use and possibly dependency."

He quickly removed the last sentence from his thought as he pictured the lady prostrate and naked in the mud knowing what damage had been done to her eye.

"Interview the people whose names were given to Owen from Valerie's parents and track those who were with Valerie for the weekend." He turned to three officers sitting together. "Scan town CCTV images for her movements on both nights. We have a time and place for the start to her Sunday evening. Check phone records also and Internet use from Cooper's address. Collect any office paper too, he's bound to have a printer." He then pointed to an officer by the door. "Shakti, interview restaurant and bar owners you know to be in the area Valerie was dropped off. I want a timeline account of their evening. Check out CCTV of all roads in the area of the murder. We have an approximate time from an eye witness. Liz, get Communications to distribute Valerie's photograph and organise the phones, if she did attend a private party someone will have seen her. Lastly, thanks very much, it's not been pleasant but I believe these two murders are in some way connected. Keep everyone informed, that means uplifting information immediately to HOLMES. (The Home Office Large Major Enquiry System). Each uplifted item will be allocated a unique message number opening a line of enquiry. The more details added will mean that the clues or coincidences won't be overlooked. Liz and Owen will co-ordinate interviews but I want them doing ASAP."

"Who'll interview her employer?" Owen asked without looking up, knowing the answer before Cyril spoke.

***

Cyril had made notes after looking through the information gleaned so far on Valerie Atkins from her professional media profile of *LinkedIn* and her *Facebook* page. Her continued career as a broadcast journalist had been successful considering the competitive nature of her chosen profession. After a work placement, post degree, with Sky and BBC television, she had worked at Stray FM, Harrogate's local radio station, dedicated to working on the hourly news bulletin. Cyril highlighted the words, *maintaining an online presence*, whatever that meant.

She also was responsible for patching news to other radio stations. He checked the list. Other police visits would be required.

Her profile as a radio personality might have attracted unwanted attention and Cyril made a note to get someone to check her social media sites to determine whether she had been targeted.

'*Blame Makes the Claim*'; Cyril slid a disc into his computer and watched the forty-minute documentary. It investigated the claim culture and highlighted a number of the aptly named ambulance chasing insurance companies that clearly undermined those working within the NHS, the teaching profession and the police. He identified Valerie, the main broadcaster and was impressed by her on screen presence and the depth of her strong yet professional interviewing technique; she seemed little fazed, asking controversial questions and forcing the interviewee onto a back foot. It was certainly cutting edge and controversial viewing. If she did not have enemies before it was broadcast, she surely would afterwards as certain companies were identified as not only morally borderline but clearly sailing close to the edge of legality. He noted the contact details of the production company, which had produced and distributed the documentary.

He picked up the phone.

"Owen, have you collected Valerie's laptop or IT equipment for analysis?"

"It hasn't been located, Sir. Wasn't at Cooper's according to her partner nor at her parents' house. Mother said it was always with her but I doubt she'd take it on a night out. Nothing other than the memory stick was found in the box."

"Her car?"

"With Forensics now but nothing of that nature found."

"I'll organise a search of Cooper's place. Any IT equipment I want analysing. Anything from her brother?"

"Wigan Police have interviewed him but he hasn't been back to Harrogate for more than six months. Told the officer that he wouldn't be returning either, not even for the funeral!"

"Not all was rosy there then? When was the last time he and Cooper met or spoke?"

"It's believed that Cooper acted somewhat unprofessionally when they worked together during their first year. The action resulted in Cooper's being given promotion over James but we're unaware of the fine details. He wouldn't say, simply suggested that it was in the past and it was, to quote, 'Blown out of all proportion'. The same year, Cooper started seeing Valerie. James left to take up work in Wigan. According to his mother, James never recovered from his sister's death. From what I understand, he was with her when she was victim of the hit and run and supposedly responsible for her when the tragedy happened, even though he was a child himself. She said he was cold emotionally like his father."

"What did she mean by that?"

"Don't know, I remember Liz's face when she heard that."

"Have we interviewed the father?"

"Tomorrow."

"See if we can get him in here so he's away from familiar ground and away from his wife… make something up, Owen. Be creative and research Jennifer's death."

***

The brass plaque was in clear need of Brasso and a degree of good old elbow grease; it was a certainly not a good first impression in Cyril's eyes. He rang the intercom and waited until a voice responded. It was if it were gargling with thick treacle.

Not understanding a word, Cyril leaned towards the small, metallic box before replying. "DCI Bennett, I have an appointment with Frederick Grant." He spoke slowly hoping the listener could understand.

The buzzer sounded and Cyril pushed the door open. The entrance hall was brightly lit. Pictures hung on either side and to his left was a stick and coat stand. Cyril was immediately attracted to the gilt-framed images, modern and abstract, adding a powerful splash of colour that contradicted artistically the Victorian, high-ceilinged hall.

"Apologies, DCI Bennett for the rather poor intercom reception, water in the wires, I believe." She raised her shoulders as if to show that the problem had been long standing. "This way please."

Cyril glanced at the stairs facing him from where the voice emanated; he noticed the female figure on the landing, semi-silhouetted by a large, stained glass window depicting a number of religious scenes.

"Beautiful windows!" Cyril stared for a moment before moving quickly up the stairs.

"The original owner bought them when they were pulling down a local church and I believe he had them fitted in the 1930s. It was during a period when visitors to Harrogate spent more time on spa treatments than on spiritual healing. That's commercialism, I suppose, one thing prospers as another withers on the vine."

Cyril looked up and in the top section of the six-panel window was a glazed, coloured image of an eye. It brought immediately to mind the prostate figure of Valerie Atkins and he cringed at the thought of the physical act of her murder; he hated coincidences, always had.

"Supposedly the eye of God, Chief Inspector, but we think it's there so that the boss can keep an eye on us." She smiled again before turning to climb the next short flight of stairs.

Cyril glanced again at the eye before following her up the last flight of stairs.

She knocked on a door before opening it. "DCI Bennett, to see you Mr Grant."

She held open the door and Cyril entered.

***

DC Shakti Misra added the requested timeline detailing Valerie's whereabouts on the Sunday evening to one of the freestanding boards in the designated Incident Room. Valerie's party had comprised five females and although they had been dropped at Pizza Express, they had neither a booking nor did they eat there. The first confirmed sighting had been in a bar on Princess Square at 18:55. The owner had remembered them for what he called their 'immature enthusiasm'. They had then moved to a bar in John Street before arriving at a Chinese Restaurant on Crescent Road. According to the restaurant's CCTV footage, two had left at 21:55 leaving Valerie with the others who had yet to be identified. They had left at 22:15. The next sighting had been by the Pump Room Museum where they could be seen crossing and heading to either the park or in the direction of Swan Road. There was no further sighting.

Shakti left an empty but accurately graded timeline until the moment in the early hours when Valerie had been spotted entering the park. She quickly checked what she had written and headed to her desk. Diligently she worked her way through the list of hotels and B and Bs situated in the vicinity of Swan Road.

Liz entered and went to look at the timeline.

"I have the names of her four university friends, Shakti. You can imagine their emotional state considering their long-standing, close relationship but all have managed to send photographs. Some can you believe, are selfies!" She added them to the board and dropped copies on Shakti's desk.

Shakti checked the CCTV footage against the four photographs and quickly eliminated Sheila Walsh and Karen Johnson as being the first to leave. Liz leaned over her shoulder and kept pointing to the screen. She checked their addresses and found one lived in Sheffield and the other in Holmfirth. The remaining two were relatively local, one from Knaresborough and the other, York.

Liz tapped her on the shoulder. "Now good old police work begins. Good luck!"

Shakti smiled whilst pulling a face. "Cheers, love."

***

Frederick Grant's office was impressive, modern and minimalist whilst complementing the high Victorian moulded plaster ceilings and the large bow window that afforded a wonderful view onto The Stray. Known as the lungs of Harrogate, it comprised two hundred acres of open, public land that is the jewel in the spa town's crown.

"Stunning view, Mr Grant, ever changing I'm sure with the seasons!"

"Never tire of it."

Cyril's eyes scanned the posters and photographs on the walls and then the statue-like silver, gold trophies and awards that were neatly lined up on the old mantelpiece above a fireplace. Fresh flowers filled the grate. He liked the order of things and relaxed slightly.

"Sad news about Valerie, Chief Inspector. I keep asking myself why someone would want to murder the poor girl." He looked directly at Cyril as if awaiting a reply.

"What was the last independent project she was working on, the one recently accepted by a television company?"

Grant shook his head. "There isn't a project. Let's say she's on leave, or was, sorry! She had success with the last production we worked on."

"*Blame Makes the Claim,*" Cyril interrupted.

"Yes, that documentary was outstanding, her own idea and her own research. She was a bright girl. She was a strong presence in front of the camera as well as on radio. The documentary was licensed to four TV channels. She thought that would herald the start of great things but like all elements of this game, it's fickle and a cruel master. One minute you can be up and everyone's friend and favourite, the next moment you're down. The 'friends' you thought you had move onto the next hot property. Remember the television personality Simon Dee?"

Cyril shook his head but made a mental note to look him up.

"Anyway, the documentary didn't find favour in everyone's eyes, upset an awful lot of folk."

Cyril noted another coincidence. *Someone found favour with one of hers,* he thought.

"People get very protective when there are compensation claims on the NHS, the armed forces, police, teachers and our public servants. I'm sure you're well aware of the Health and Safety issues that clearly restrict the way we all go about our work, Chief Inspector. Litigation is rife, it's commercial, it's big business but it's catastrophic at the same time. It restricts challenge, daring and what life is about, risk!" He paused. "Sorry, since we worked on the programme it's really had an effect on my perception of the parasitic lawyers. Valerie was simply presenting a point of view for the audience to consider but TV can make personalities and the personalities get the praise but also the hatred. If you put your head above the parapet you have to accept that it can be shot at."

"And was it shot at?"

"Bloody hell, yes! Producing controversial stuff is like putting a stick into a hornets' nest."

Cyril looked up as he said that and whether it was Cyril's quizzical expression or his sudden physical response, it made him pause.

"Have I said something wrong?"

"Interesting simile. No, sorry, continue, it was what you just said that brought something to mind. Please…"

"Where was I?"

"Hornets' nest," Cyril responded.

"Yes… hornets. She received a good deal of flak, but also a good deal of professional commendation. Nominated for a couple of awards. The TV people loved it, she was the best thing since the sliced loaf, but as you can imagine there were members of the public and certain businesses who, quite frankly, made it personal. Anyway it affected her in several ways. She was, at the time the documentary came out, working at Stray FM but her deadlines and presentation became a little, shall we say to be fair to her, erratic. You can't have that emotional instability on live radio so she was side-lined, given 'leave' to get herself together."

"How long has she been with the agency, Mr Grant?"

"We put her on our books not long after university. We took her on trust. She was very confident and had made up a show-reel, not professional, but you could clearly see her potential. We gave her more on-reel experience, more, shall we say, exposure. In the early days we helped her to get that."

Cyril's mind went back to the naked female prostrated over a table when he heard the word 'exposure'.

"She became a kind of featured expert on some local, television morning shows dealing with youth issues. She was professional and knew her stuff. You might have seen a few; one in particular was on children being unnecessarily prescribed the drug Ritalin. It was shown about eight months back. It's only brief but… I have a copy if you…"

"Don't have a television, Mr Grant," Cyril interrupted. He held out a hand. "For evidence, it will be viewed. Was she a drug user?"

The lack of reaction to such a sensitive question surprised Cyril. He had assumed that that such an enquiry coming out of the blue would cause a degree of surprise. He was clearly wrong.

"Couldn't say, but I personally never experienced that in all the time I represented her. What I will say is that there is a culture of drug use within this profession and that includes an over reliance on alcohol. Seems to go hand in glove, Chief Inspector. I can also confirm that she liked a party and loved a drink."

"Did she get herself together after the pressure she received from the documentary?"

"We managed to get her some broadcasting work in York and she seemed to pick up. She quickly became more her professional self. Believe me, Chief Inspector, when she was on form she was bloody brilliant. I don't act for numpties, as you can witness from the successes here." He pointed to the awards.

"When did you last see, Valerie?"

He flicked open his desk diary and scanned the page. "Monday's today, yes?" After licking his finger he turned back the pages. "Here, last Wednesday. Popped in as I'd organised a voice-over audition, local studio for a radio advert. Bit of a pot boiler but if you can get them, you take them. There are more and more these days what with social media advertising." He rubbed his finger and thumb together. "Pays very well for very little effort."

Cyril looked across the desk at Frederick Grant and noted the armpit sweat marks that had appeared like two shadows of guilt on his shirt.

"Did she do it?"

"Sorry?"

"The voice over?"

"No. Tomorrow, sadly I've had to offer it to another client."

"So she never mentioned her new project to you when she saw you?"

Grant shook his head. "I can't believe that she'd go behind my back and work independently or with another agency, we'd known each other too long."

"I'll need a list of your media contacts, all of them, Mr Grant, your clients too and those you represent. I note that some are listed on your website but not all. We know that she'd been accepted to work on a new documentary but at this stage we don't know by whom. One of my officers will call in this afternoon. I'm sure you'll have all the relevant names and addresses ready."

Cyril never let his face slip as he stood and motioned to leave. He stopped at the door before turning to face Grant. "Thank you for your full co-operation in this murder enquiry. Lovely cool office you have, too. I'll see myself out." He then afforded Grant a short smile.

If Frederick Grant had been unaware of the severity of the investigation and his part in it, then Cyril Bennett wanted to leave him in no doubt that he would be investigated fully.

As Cyril arrived at the top of the stairs, he glanced at the stained-glass eye. For some unknown reason he wondered if it were God's left or right eye that was watching his every move as he approached the landing. *Suppose it depends on whether he was left or right handed*, he thought as he opened the door to leave. At the same time, Frederick Grant wiped his forehead before removing a mobile phone from the top drawer of his desk.

Chapter Seven

John Cooper sat in the waiting area of Harrogate Police Station. It was 16:35. His left foot bounced involuntarily as if catching the beat of some inaudible tune. Owen watched him on the security camera before going to meet him. Although it was a voluntary interview, he would be cautioned and it would still be recorded. Owen was at great pains to explain his rights to Cooper, emphasising the relevance of the interview and that he was free to go whenever he chose.

Computer equipment taken from the house had revealed nothing of relevance and the phone records of both Cooper and Valerie had shown no out of the ordinary variation. Owen had decided that his questioning would follow three strands at this point: their relationship, her professional career and his relationship with her brother, James. If anything further were to be revealed then he would pursue that also.

Leaving a trail of droplets on the floor, Owen collected two polystyrene cups of coffee and went into Interview Room Four. He left the door ajar.

"As I've said, Mr Cooper, you control this chat. We can stop at any time you feel distressed or too upset to continue; we are aware of the difficulties you face. We must, however, remember that we're working together, we're chasing your partner's murderer and the more information we can get at this stage, the better chance we have of catching him or her."

"Her?" John Cooper lifted his head up.

Owen just lifted his shoulders. "Not all murderers are men, Mr Cooper, not by a long way."

"Mr Cooper, how long have you known Valerie?" Owen sipped his coffee trying to help the man who appeared a bundle of emotional nerves to relax.

"I met her through James, her brother. We were both working in the same school. I'd been there a year when he arrived. We got on well, same interests with teaching the same subject. It just grew from there. It's been five years…" He stopped to think before forcing a smile. "Five years on December 19th. He brought her to a school production."

"When did you start living together?"

"Pretty much straight away. She was pleased to get away from home. Still goes back, she runs away from conflict, the smallest row she just goes home for a couple of days and then returns as if nothing's happened. Considering the intensity of her job and the way she's so determined to extract the truth on camera, it has to be said that her professional life belies her true self. She's very naïve, Sergeant."

"What do you know about her latest independent project? We heard that she's just had a new television commission accepted."

"God! She was so thrilled. She'd had great success previously with a documentary and she thought she'd made the grade but things went quiet. Suffered a lot of social media animosity, too. She'd expected some backlash but when it came, boy did it come! It wouldn't have been the programme it was if it hadn't divided some elements of the viewing public. Many still crucified her though. Consequently, she suffered a severe bout of depression. Have you ever seen or known a sufferer?" He didn't give Owen chance to answer. "Bloody dreadful, they close in on themselves and reject any kind of help. I told her to look at the positives in her life and to remember the praise she received, but that made matters even worse. I now know it was totally the wrong approach. It's like watching someone drowning and although you can reach them, they reject your hand almost deliberately submerging themselves. It's heart-breaking! She'd suffered before when her sister was killed but that was way back, before I knew her."

He put his head down and sipped his coffee. Owen waited hoping the pause would make him expand.

"Do you know something that's bloody strange? One minute she could be the life and soul and then the next minute she could be dragging herself from the deepest and darkest of places."

"Was she on medication?"

"Venlafaxine, I think it is. There'll be tablets in the kitchen cupboard but her GP will give you all the details. I think she was on Prozac too at some stage. For the last six to eight months she's been very positive and with the acceptance of her latest project, she was truly bubbling with excitement." He paused and drank the remnants of his coffee. "You asked about the project, didn't you? Sorry! I've seen nothing other than the working title she had; she turned the laptop round one evening and showed me. She'd typed, '*Modern Day Farming*'. When she showed me she laughed as if it were some great conundrum or riddle. I think she said that I'd never guess what it was really about but that it would make everyone sit up."

Owen pulled a face; he was rather taken aback by the title before writing it down and repeating it. "And you don't know what it's about? Had she been visiting local farms?"

Cooper shook his head. "She could be very secretive. Sometimes I wondered if she were making it all up, kind of a false hope but she was unfathomable when she was like that. Sadly, I don't think she understood herself."

"Do you still see her brother?"

"He moved away, Wigan, I think. We had a fall out over exam marking, stupid really and very mundane. He accused me of cheating, suggesting wrongly that I guided my students' course work in order to gain higher pass percentages for them. He threatened to approach the School's Governors. I don't think he did, didn't have the facts nor the bottle. Shortly afterwards, we both applied for the post of Second in Department and I was successful. He resigned from his position and moved away. Neither seen nor heard from him since!"

"Last question and thanks for your honesty." Owen smiled. "Did either of you enjoy recreational drugs?"

John Cooper put his head down and laughed. "You want me to incriminate myself, Sergeant?" He paused and looked Owen straight in the eye. "Haven't we all?"

Owen returned his eye contact and felt himself nodding.

"Yes, bit of grass, the odd tablet but for me very little. I tend to like to be in control of my faculties, besides drugs and education don't make good bedfellows. I love my job and don't want to lose it."

"Valerie?"

"Same."

"Thanks very much, Mr Cooper, you've been most helpful. Has Ruth Jones been looking after you?"

When Owen mentioned Ruth's name, a pressure seemed to suddenly evaporate from the atmosphere in the room, bringing a smile to John Cooper's lips.

"Thanks, yes. Helping me get things organised. She's enabling me come to terms with the situation. She explained about the Coroner and when Val's body might be released. She's good at her job, Sergeant, bloody good and I'm grateful for her support, thanks."

Owen simply nodded. "Murder cases take time but we all want the same outcome… we want justice for Valerie."

John looked back at Owen. "I'd kill the bastard myself, that would be my kind of justice."

Owen didn't respond, he simply stood and escorted him out of the building.

It was remarkably quiet once outside. Owen stood at the top of the steps that looked down onto the small car park. The Mini Cooper's rasp broke the stillness of the early evening before heading towards the station entrance. Owen took a deep breath and stretched; he felt tired. Through the trees that bordered the police building from the road, he could see a line of smudged, turquoise light that formed the eastern horizon. The subtle colour blended swiftly into the autumn evening's dark until it completely vanished. He wondered why Valerie had kept all her loved ones in ignorance of her latest project. Was she frightened of the content or was she simply protecting them from her own disappointment, the truth being that there was no actual documentary and no offer? Maybe the project was purely a figment of her disturbed imagination. He wondered if the truth would ever really be discovered or whether it would simply vanish like the subtle, evening light.

"Beer?"

Owen turned. It was Liz.

"Deep in thought then big fella. If you want a beer it's your round."

"I'll be five minutes."

Chapter Eight

Cyril sat in Dr Julie Pritchett's office for only a few minutes before the mystical objects trapped in jars or displayed loosely on the shelves attracted him like a child to a sweet shop window. Ever since he had first met her in this very room, he had been fascinated by the motley collection and, on occasion had been repulsed by the various anatomical specimens she had amassed. He noted that at the far end of the bottom shelf was an item that he had not seen before. He bent down looking at the white ribbon-like object trapped within a tall, transparent jar. He did not hear her enter.

"Taenia Solium, Cyril. You really don't want one!"

Cyril turned and smiled. "Tapeworm, if I'm not mistaken?"

"Correct, Sherlock, but which one?"

"Don't know but what I do know is that your shelves still need a good dusting."

"From pork. They can live inside their host for thirty years and grow to lengths of twenty-six feet. Need a lot of feeding!" She smiled and sat down. "Dust- free offices and tidy desks… Listen to your doctor… they are both the sign of a sick mind."

Cyril just pulled a face; he could not tolerate either.

"I bet your mother used to clean the house at midnight before you went on holiday, too, just in case the bus crashed and some strangers would have to go in! I can hear them now… E*e, Mrs Bennett were proper house proud, not a speck o' dust! Such a shame! Do ya think anyone 'll notice if I nicked that vase?*"

Cyril just pulled another face and blushed a little at the truth. "No complaints, Julie, no complaints."

She realised she had trodden on ground that was a little too personal and moved on quickly.

"Now, Cyril, the reason for your visit. The toxicology results for Valerie Atkins are here. Isaac Caner has asked me to talk you through them. He also wants to see you about some further findings." She turned the computer screen round. "Make interesting reading too! There's a fair old list: Valium, marijuana, mephedrone, as well as her prescription drug, Venlafaxine. She'd suffered from depression since the death of her sister and according to her GP, she's had a bit of an emotional roller coaster these last couple of years. The prescribed dosage has fluctuated over time depending on her need. She was drug dependent looking at the tests on brain and liver samples. It's frightening how quickly physical dependency can result when Diazepam is abused."

"If she was already being treated for depression with medication why take Diazepam?"

"Gives a feeling of euphoria, like feeling a little drunk. It helps you to forget for a while. Trouble is, when the withdrawal kicks in, you suffer further anxiety, irritation, which leads to greater depression. That leads to further drug abuse, that's why we find mephedrone and the like. Vicious circle, Cyril, but when she's hooked, she's hooked. We also found traces of Ketamin. It's an anaesthetic, taken to help you forget, but at the same time it can render the taker extremely vulnerable and out of control. It's said that it pushes away your problems for a while. You'll know it as the date rape drug and from my medical perspective it's incongruous, why would she take something like that? She wouldn't! In my opinion it's been carefully administered to her."

"Amnesia?"

Julie nodded. "Exactly, debilitating. So for someone who liked to be in control, it would be anathema to her in my opinion."

"We know she'd arranged to meet someone so what you're saying contradicts that. She could have allowed herself to be totally manipulated. When she was dropped off, she might have had no recollection of what had happened to her or where she'd been and possibly with whom. We know for a fact that an eye-witness noted that she was a little unsteady as she came down the road shortly before she was murdered."

"Possible. The previous occasions she had found her way home or was taken home but on this occasion that wasn't the case, other plans may have been made. This was possibly the only time the drug was given; there was a change in the rules or she'd broken them."

"What about the videos?"

"I've seen them, all four, and she appears to be in charge of all her faculties during the filming. I assume that they were consensual, she was clearly a willing participant. However, you can't discard a more sinister element on this occasion, one that she had no control over whatsoever."

"Evidence of sexual abuse?"

"Some vaginal scarring but nothing to suggest anything too bizarre, possible rough, over-enthusiastic intercourse. No evidence of anal damage, which quite surprised me. She'd had sex the night she died. Testing at the moment."

Cyril rubbed his chin. "None of the drugs taken was directly responsible for her death we have to remember. She was murdered and murdered very brutally."

"I'm only furnishing you with the evidence. I'll leave the pipe, magnifying glass and bloodhound-on-a-string sleuthing to you and your able team." She stood. "Other bodies demand my attention."

She came round the desk, smiled and gave him a peck on the cheek. "Ring me and I don't mean next week, Cyril… And Cyril… Bring your duster next time." She blew him a kiss and went to leave. "And don't forget, Caner wants to see you!"

Cyril stood and followed her to the door. He ran his finger along the nearest shelf leaving a clean line, before she turned right and he left. The walls of the corridor were glass panelled and although certain rooms were closed from scrutiny with venetian blinds, others remained fascinatingly open. He glanced at the white, lab-coated figures huddled together. He then noticed Caner. He paused. Caner spied Cyril in the corridor and waved a hand holding up two fingers.

Another inappropriate greeting, Cyril reflected and smiled.

Caner appeared at the door, a light blue, bouffant cap covering his hair. He held up his gloved hands. "Thanks for stopping by, Cyril. Two things. Julie talked you through the Toxicology, yes?"

Cyril nodded.

"Good. Your killer is left handed, no doubt. We tracked the trajectory of the steel by analysing the way the tape covering her eyes responded to the force of the initial insertion. Left handed." Caner smiled. "If you'll excuse me, just doing more tests. Will forward as soon as." He returned to the group.

***

Owen stood in the Incident Room and stared at the timeline Shakti had drawn. He sipped tea from his new mug. There were four brown tide-lines from the lip to the surface of the tea, clearly dating the last time the mug had been washed. He read the notes from the interviews Liz had held with Sheila Walsh and Karen Johnson, occasionally referencing the times against the markers on the wall. They reported that Valerie had simply been Valerie over the weekend, fun loving, jovial and as usual, slightly 'pissed'. She had displayed no real anxiety throughout the whole of their time together. He noted that both friends had made references to her successes but nothing had been said of her failures. Neither had volunteered that she had suffered from depression nor that she had any medical issues. He turned to Shakti.

"What of the other two?"

"It's worth noting that they were all, apart from Nancy, partakers in recreational drugs, Marijuana mainly but the occasional cocaine. University habit only. They emphasised that they are occasional users, touch nothing for weeks. It was clear that Valerie had supplied them this weekend but it was with very little… allegedly."

As she spoke, Shakti turned to her computer and her fingers danced across the keyboard.

"Nancy Anders… lives in York. She was the last to see Valerie. They had all stayed at The Croft Hotel. Two checked out Sunday but Anders and Gough were checking out on the Monday morning so the three went back to their rooms after the meal. Valerie stayed until just before midnight. They said she'd organised a taxi. Nancy reported seeing her get into a car and then they both went to bed. She was, they say, slightly, and I quote, *pissed*."

"None of them thought that she was acting any differently from previous weekend dos?'

"Their weekend soirées?"

Owen pulled a face and raised an eyebrow, making a mental note of the word. He'd look it up later.

"No. Anders and Gough checked out together at…" She checked for the time. "08:15, neither took breakfast. Nancy dropped Gail Gough in Knaresborough on her way."

"CCTV?"

"From the hotel Reception. No sign of Valerie leaving but we see them arrive and the check out times all correspond."

"Any other camera footage?"

"Sorry!"

"Are you checking their social media accounts?"

"In hand but I've only two of these and you're occupying them!" She lifted her hands and waggled her fingers. She then smiled. "Passed it to the Techy people."

Owen grinned, sipped more tea and moved to the boards.

***

Cyril typed the name *Simon Dee* into Google and read the Wikipedia entry. He was initially shocked that they shared the same Christian name, Cyril; Simon Dee being his stage name. He was also surprised to learn that he too had been aradio and television interviewer for a time and on more than one occasion had fallen out with his employers before eventually spending time in prison. It was after reading about the blonde model and the E-Type Jaguar that he vaguely remembered the programme. Grant had obviously seen the similarities in both Dee's and Valerie's career paths but why had he not stepped in with more support? Why had he no recollection of her planning a new project when he knew that she was fragile? Surely part of his role would be to safeguard her professional welfare. He then thought of the video Liz had presented and her words came back to him... *none of the men has been identified, they were each different in every video.* Could one of them have been Grant?

He flipped open the file on Frederick Grant and was surprised by the date of birth recorded. Cyril thought he looked older than forty-eight. There was something about him that he had taken a growing dislike to and the one thing that he now relied on was to always trust his gut feelings. He read the file further until an incoming email announced itself, breaking his concentration. Cyril read it.

Semen sample found: No fit to DNA or John Cooper or samples stored. Checking National DNA database for a possible match using familial search.

The familial search would trawl the NDNAD to check against DNA samples from a relative with a similar match, which in turn might give a lead. Cyril marked it as noted and continued reading Grant's file. He checked the agency's web site, aptly named, *Stray Agency*. It brought a smile to his face. It was typical advertising speak but the details of Grant's history corresponded with the notes on file.

17 years' experience managing the careers of top newsreaders and hard-hitting investigative journalists across a wide...

Cyril checked the names of about ten on the list. Valerie Atkins was midfield. He brought up her page. Her image appeared and a brief, professional biography. He did the same for all the clients but there was nothing that drew his attention. He returned to the home page before reverting to the police file. What he needed was to see all the connections the Stray Agency had with the media at large and although he had strong feelings about Grant, he felt the business was legitimate.

Chapter Nine

The large, Yorkshire stone, Victorian building that was now an auction house was five minutes' walk from the centre of Ilkley. Sylvia Bentham parked her car and collected a ticket from the machine to leave on the dashboard. A rather rotund, female parking warden watched from a few cars away and nodded when she had placed it securely. There was no smile. She had given herself one hour. She checked her watch before removing a small, boxed package from the boot.

Although the day was fine, she felt the chill wind moving from high on the moors before channelling itself through lanes and ginnels; even with her collar pulled up it seemed to have little effect. She smiled at being without a hat in this part of Yorkshire. The sky hung grey and cloudless, offering little in the way of hospitality. The traffic, however, was light as she crossed Brook Street from West Street and from there she made good progress. Her appointment was for 11:45 and she glanced again at her watch. The last thing she wanted was to be too early.

Colin Crompton was waiting behind Reception and he immediately came to the counter as she entered. "Mrs Bentham?" He smiled, more in anticipation than in greeting. It had been a long morning and he had felt his stomach rumble on more than one occasion. He was hoping that he could value the items quickly and then enjoy a leisurely lunch.

"Mr Crompton?" She saw him nod and his smile broadened even more. "I hope I'm not too early? I have them here." She lifted the box.

Colin led her upstairs to the main gallery and found a table surrounded by a number of ill-matching chairs. The hall was full of items collected over the preceding days in readiness for the next specialist November Fine Art auction; to the untrained eye there seemed to be no logic to the way they were stored. They sat.

"It's proving to be a popular sale, we've some wonderful silver which will help your items should you decide to enter them for auction."

She opened the package and put two Charles Horner silver hatpins on the table followed by a small oil painting.

"I thought you only had the silver pins?" His smile said he was now neither in a hurry nor thinking about food. "Those are in lovely condition, Art Deco in style. My auction estimate would be in the region of £80 to £120. Bit of an auctioneer's cliché I'm afraid!"

She looked at him and smiled. "The painting is probably not worth much but I thought I'd bring it whilst I was coming."

The auctioneer picked up the painting. "On the contrary, it's worth considerably…"

He popped a jeweller's loop to his eye and scanned the image. Somewhere in the room a large clock chimed noon but went decidedly tuneless after striking five and died after striking nine.

"Needs a little TLC like us all," he chuckled, removing the loop. "Someone will buy it and bring its chimes back to life. I believe this to be an oil sketch by the late Italian artist, Migliaro. His signature is clear. It looks to be painted on panel too, which is right for this type of painting, probably a preparatory work for a large oil painting. I'll have to check on that. I believe it may well be worth more than you think. I should like our Fine Art expert to cast her eye on it if that's all right? Have you had it long?"

She had hoped that the painting would be the focus of attention and that she would be remembered more for that than the pins. "No, it's like everything else, a car boot find. I'm an early bird, Mr Crompton. Surprising what people think of as junk. Things soon go out of fashion and they throw them away."

"Yes, I think it could do very well. I shouldn't but may I ask what you paid at the car boot for the painting?"

"Two pounds. He wanted five but I haggled. Even if you sell it for a hundred it would be very welcome. I'll leave it with you and telephone you next week. Shall I ask for you or…?"

"Ask for Joanna Murphy, she'll talk you through her impressions and discuss an estimate and then if you're happy it can find its level at auction."

Ten minutes later, she was heading back to the car. She had a receipt for the two pins and a separate receipt for the painting. *How many people would touch those items before November?* She wondered. She too now, suddenly, felt as though she could eat something, her anxiety had suddenly dissipated and her appetite had returned.

***

The Ford Transit van waited at the top of Sand's Road. The North Sea was directly below and in front of them, invisible but faintly audible. The time was 02:49. The rain drove gently but consistently at the windscreen and occasionally the wipers were activated to clear the view. The engine remained silent. The Rib, the small, rigid boat should have dropped the four pieces of human contraband on the sand on the last high tide at 01:45; unheard and unseen. They had been instructed where to wait.

The driver checked his watch again and it was then that he saw movement as people appeared out of the darkness. Quickly, he jumped out and opened the side door and four bedraggled female figures were pushed in without ceremony.

"Fucking freezin' down there!" the escorting figure exclaimed, rubbing his hands. "Piss wet through! Jesus and when I was a kid I imagined smugglers to be these jolly fellas havin' fun at the expense of the fat customs' men. Brandy for Parson, baccy for the Clerk and all that shite! Nothing written about freezin' your bollocks off whilst four females huddle together who you can't fucking touch."

The two waiting in the van laughed before the only female of the three announced, "I'll sit with the girls."

Within half an hour the van had pulled off onto a narrow lane running almost parallel with the main road, clearly signed 'Unsuitable for Motor Vehicles'. Half way along, they were expecting the rendezvous. On this occasion the appointed meeting place was Flixton, one of the many villages that was used as a transfer point along the route from the coast.

As planned, the blue Range Rover was waiting, silently invisible in the gateway. Within seconds the cargo was switched. By 04:00 both vehicles would be safely stored, nobody would be the wiser but some would be financially richer and some, a lot warmer.

***

Cyril's walk to the station was just what he needed and for once there was neither rain nor the prospect of rain for the morning, at least according to the radio forecast. It would give him time to collect his thoughts. He turned left as he exited the snicket at the end of Robert Street before heading towards the Otley Road roundabout; a dog barked as it chased a ball along the edge of The Stray. He stopped briefly and watched the animal's skill as it swiftly caught the ball. His mind focused on the derelict portal of the Brunswick Tunnel as he recalled a previous case. He closed his eyes to rid himself of the sinister image.

As he approached the roundabout there was a light mist that swallowed the upper part of Trinity Methodist Church spire. The morning was quite dark. Lights along the far side of The Stray were still lit. He checked his watch, shook it and looked again. It was 07:35. The walk would normally take thirty minutes. He slipped his electronic cigarette into his mouth and pressed the button on the side; a white cloud of vapour blended effortlessly with the morning mist as he set off at quite a pace.

On his arrival, the Incident Room was busy, the hum of conversation hanging thickly like an alphabet soup of tangled words. When Cyril entered it fell to silence.

"Morning everyone."

"Sir." The reply was almost choral.

"Five minutes. Get what you need."

Cyril worked his way down the boards and looked at the details of the timeline. He turned to Shakti, smiled and raised a thumb. She returned the smile with a degree of embarrassment. He mingled with the group speaking to a number of officers before taking a seat next to Owen at the end of a long table. Cyril tapped the desk and everyone settled.

"Let's work through in order."

The process was slow but deliberate. Each offered information and cross-referenced it with other evidence. It then came back to Cyril.

"Pathologist is adamant that the killer is left handed. Open mind everyone. Valerie Atkins, a drug addict but may have been manipulated on the night she died. Ketamine found in her system but no evidence of rape, evidence of recent sexual activity; DNA tells us that it wasn't with Cooper, her partner. We know that she was an enthusiastic participant from the videos and there are no physical indications to suggest that it wasn't consensual. Open mind again, please. Valerie's computers, anything?"

"Nothing yet, Sir."

Cyril nodded at Stuart Park. "What about Coulson's?"

The technicians at the High-tech Crime Unit have been great again. After receiving the full reports, I called them and they broke the info down into simple terms for me."

"I'll send thanks to Newby Wiske." Cyril made a note.

"Thanks, best to keep on their side, Sir. Right, here goes and I'll ask questions at the end, Liz, so stay awake!"

He had never forgotten the first briefing she had given when she had put friendly pressure on him and when possible, he always took the opportunity to return the compliment.

Liz smiled and raised herself a little from a slouch to a half loll. "All ears!"

"Coulson was Internet savvy. Used Tor Proxy Browser provider allowing him to send traffic through at least three different servers before it reached its final destination. This gave a separate level of encryption for each of the three relays. It protected his location and gave him full anonymity, securing him from traffic analysis. The police use a similar system, as do the Armed Forces. What's good for the goose is very useful for the gander. He also used a password manager. Like everything in life there is an Achilles' heel and that's usually human frailty. Three days before he was murdered, he sent out some open messages without activating his security. They were brief and he soon realised his error. There's evidence that he tried to delete them in the hope that they wouldn't be tracked but the likelihood is that whoever saw them was able to locate him. If you're fighting with the big boys you've got to be aware that their systems and skills will be better. We can't find who they might have been. It's likely that this one simple error exposed him to harm."

"Do we know what the open messages were?"

"Yes, they were berating the production and distribution of cannabis in the UK. Some touched on the illegal use of migrants but in the main they were focussed on the trade in home-grown drugs." Stuart tapped the large screen and the first message appeared. "He's added the first two letters of three names but that's all. They're the same on each of the messages. Techies also found three photographs; it took a while to crack the password system."

Stuart skimmed through the three images. Each showed the hydroponic cultivation of large quantities of cannabis.

"Do we know when and where these were taken?" Owen asked, knowing the answer before he had even asked the question.

"No."

"May we assume the same can be said for Valerie Atkins's computer if we locate it? Is it likely to be similarly secure?"

There was silence.

"Until we find it, Sir, who knows?"

Owen pulled a face. "Whatever this new project was, there's a link." He flicked through the file in front of him. "Cooper mentioned that the working title of the documentary or whatever it was she was working on was… *'Modern Day Farming'*. Certainly in this modern day every urban area has some shed, loft, flat turned into a greenhouse, producing the stuff. Let's assume we're heading in the right direction but with something on an industrial, farm-size scale let's say."

Cyril nodded and made a note before adding his comments.

"Frederick Grant is adamant that he knew nothing of his client's new documentary. It wasn't, he assured me, commissioned through his agency. Liz will be going through a contact list and documents collected from the Agency to see if Valerie was working independently or with another agent. I feel Grant is saying little more than he needs to. What about Valerie's father?"

"Heartbroken. Cried a lot. Couldn't understand why his daughter should have been murdered. He used the words, '*Taken from him.*' Certainly didn't appear to be the cold and clinical character his wife made him out to be. You can never predict what's going to happen to your emotions in situations like this. He was of little help. It seems Valerie only allowed them into certain parts of her life."

"Did she witness her sister's death? Was she there when the accident happened?" Cyril stood and stretched.

Owen checked through the file. "Yes, she was, She was eleven and Jennifer was seven."

Cyril moved to a white board that was to the left of the screen.

"I was thinking over a beer last night. A dangerous thing to do I know, the process of both murders and pieces of key evidence that we hold brought a very special person to mind. Here's your starter for ten. Please say what comes to mind."

He picked up a marker and began writing:

"There are moments when I feel that the Shylocks, the Judases, and even the Devil are broken spokes in the great wheel of good which shall in due time be made whole."

There was silence.

"What did the murderer take from Coulson?" He looked around the room at a number of blank faces. He saw Shakti smile. "Shakti?"

"His bicycle wheel." She then paused watching the encouragement written across Cyril's face. "It was taken from the bike and dumped near the body, maybe a sign; there were spokes missing but the integrity of the wheel remained. They also took away his sense of touch, they removed his fingers."

"They? Interesting that you believe there's more than one killer."

"What was taken from Valerie?"

"Her sight." Liz squeaked, as she sat and focussed on the whiteboard.

Cyril nodded. "And what else?"

Owen waved his chewed pencil. "I believe that the murderer took two more things, one of which was tangible."

Cyril nearly choked on fresh air when he heard Owen utter the word *tangible*, not because he'd used the word but because it was in the correct context. "Go on."

"He took their dignity, the murderer left them naked and exposed but took, as Shakti has said, five tangible objects, the bicycle spokes; and so he took away…" Owen pointed to the white board. "The Shylocks, the Judases and the Devil. The question now is will he return them? Who might the Shylocks, the Judases and the Devil be?" He shoved the pencil back into his mouth and sat back. "Or do we have Shylock and Judas dead and, if so, are we waiting to find another body, that of the Devil?"

Cyril clapped his hands and a few others followed suit before Owen brought everything back down to earth with one sentence.

"That's providing…" He pointed to the whiteboard. "that, those words have any relevance to the murders or any aspect of this case. I think we're clutching at straws or spokes in this case if you prefer. As you've rightly pointed out, Sir, dangerous thing, thinking over a beer!"

There was a pause and all eyes turned to Cyril. Some heads nodded in agreement.

"You're maybe right, Owen, but Helen Keller suffered from being blind, deaf and dumb. Many senses were taken from her but she still managed to become a most extraordinary human being. She overcame all her disabilities and disadvantages at a time when that was nigh on impossible. Has our murderer done that? The murderer discovered someone in a sense hiding before taking away the sense that allowed him to communicate. The murderer removed the sight of another who threatened to use the visual arts to attack… is he trying to suggest that he has suffered but is now…"

Cyril looked around and could denote a waning of enthusiasm for his theory and he stopped. "It was a thought. Please keep an open mind, that's all I ask."

Chapter Ten

Liz had finished her review of the documents retained within a large, cardboard box collected from the Stray Agency. As a result, she contacted the television companies affiliated with Grant but with little success. She had found only one nugget from sifting through the paperwork and put it to one side. It was a screenshot of an email sent to Grant from a person that, considering the initials, she presumed to be, John Cooper. It simply stated:

Leave it! Leave Val alone; please give her time, no more pressure.
This is neither a threat nor a polite request I'm just thinking about your wellbeing as well as hers!
JC

She looked again, confused by the contrasting emotions that were evident within the short statement; in some ways it clearly posed a number of questions, but in other ways it made no sense at all. However, to one person, it might have a clearer implication.

***

Liz sat outside Copper's house; the Mini was on the drive. She scanned the building quickly. The bedroom window was ajar but the curtains were drawn as were the lounge blinds. It was 11:30. Cooper had been granted compassionate leave so he would not be in school. Ruth checked her watch.

"Shall I ring him or do you want to just knock?"

Liz opened the car door. "Christ, let's just do it. I hate pussy footing about."

Ruth knocked on the door as loudly as possible, ignoring the bell positioned to the left. She had tried it on the previous visit and had received no answer, it was probably broken. Liz stood back from the door watching for any movement of the curtains. She smiled when she saw it. At first there was just a flicker; there was definitely a twitch, then she first saw the fingers and then a gap appearing half way up.

"We have lift off!" she excitedly called to Ruth, emphasising each word. "Probably one too many last night!"

Liz watched a face appear within the gaping curtains and then a small glimmer of recognition followed as he focused on Ruth. He raised a hand as if to wave. The curtains fell closed again.

"He's alive, just. I definitely saw him move a limb!" Liz smiled at Ruth. "Looks bloody rough though, poor chap. Let's hope I don't make his day any worse." Liz's smile was more cruel than kind.

Within minutes the door opened.

"Sorry, Christ!" He rubbed his face. "I was miles away. Took a couple of the tablets the doctor prescribed to help me sleep; feel as though I've been hit by a bloody tram! What's the time?"

"After eleven. Any alcohol involved with the tablets, John?"

"Some…" He looked at Ruth's face. "I know, I know, but…" He stood back from the door and swayed slightly as he walked down the corridor. "Hopefully, you'll never have to know what it's like. I need a brew. Anyone else?"

"Sit with the sergeant and I'll do the honours. Liz?"

Liz shook her head and sat. John wrapped the dressing gown firmly around him as he took the chair opposite.

"I presume this visit isn't to check on my welfare. Have you discovered something?"

"What was your relationship like with Frederick Grant?"

"Val's agent?"

Liz simply nodded.

John pulled a face suggesting indifference. "He was her agent. We met a few times, seemed like a nice enough guy; always encouraged her, guided her career well if I were to be honest. Val wasn't always the easiest person to work with. Why?"

"Encouraged? Did he ever put pressure on her to complete work or to take certain jobs or commissions? You'll have to forgive me, the world in which your partner worked is alien to me and I'm on a steep learning curve."

"Like all bosses, pressure is their bread and butter, you get pressured they get it from their superiors. Must happen in the police too? Val said not, he appeared to understand her. She stayed with him for a long time. He was aware of her fragility after some of the criticism she received from her one real success. Ironically, the documentary was both a blessing and then a curse."

Ruth came in with his tea and sat down to the side as if totally neutral.

"Brought you a biscuit too. The sugar will give you a boost. Eat it and drink some tea, Liz has the time."

Liz sat back. "If you can you should get yourself out for some fresh air, even with the weather being as it is, blow away the cobwebs, clear your mind."

John ate the Tunnock's wafer in two bites and then put down his tea. He began to fold the foil wrapper neatly as if completing some origami exercise.

Liz couldn't help herself but filled the moment of pause by trying to recall how many million bars were allegedly sold every week according to the wrapper. She decided on six million before she noticed that John had regained a little more focus. Ruth had done well.

"John, did you ever contact him without Val's knowledge?"

There was a pause as he drank more tea and then he nodded. "Yes, on more than one occasion." He noticed she wanted more and so before she asked, he continued. "Menial tasks usually, dropping off scripts, letters, taking a bottle and card at Christmas and on his birthday, usually when I noted that she'd forgotten, that kind of visit. Sometimes I'd see him and other times I'd see Christina, his secretary and general dog's body. She's not been there that long, Grant called her his new personal assistant; pretentious in the extreme in my opinion but she was always dashing everywhere for him that's why occasionally I worried for Val. The woman she replaced left after working for him for about nine months. I thought he might have roaming bloody hands!"

"Valerie was never affected by that, I take it otherwise, she wouldn't have stayed as long as she did?"

John just shook his head whilst raising his shoulders.

"I have a copy of an email you sent. It's dated three weeks ago." She handed him a copy.

He studied it. "Not this soldier. I've never sent him an email. You've had my laptop so if it came from there you'd know, also the address, surely?"

Liz instinctively knew that he was telling the truth even though she knew it could have been sent from his phone.

"Besides it's signed JC. Could be anyone."

"Specifically about your partner. If you add two and two together, Mr Cooper."

"To a mathematics' dyslexic, two and two can make 569! I didn't send an email to Frederick Grant. I've never sent an email to Frederick Grant and now I've no reason to send an email to Grant! How much clearer do I have to make myself before you believe me?"

Ruth threw Liz a glance of concern.

Sorry, I was…" She collected herself. "It's another lead I must pursue. Thanks. Hope you feel a little brighter as the day goes on."

"I'll be a few minutes, Liz. I'll see you by the car."

Liz stood leaving Ruth with John. Her responsibility was split and Liz knew that her priority was his welfare. When she got to the car she took out her mobile and called Shakti. The rain had started again and she slipped into the driver's seat.

"Shakti, Liz. Can you arrange an appointment with Frederick Grant as soon as, today if possible? Ta! Can you also get someone to look through anything from Coulson's files or Internet traffic for anyone signing JC." She turned and saw Ruth leave the house.

"I know his system was as tight as the proverbial but just in case. I'll await your call."

Ruth opened the car door. "More tears I'm afraid. Only natural, I've warned him about the booze. Also told him to contact any nearest and dearest, try and get away for a couple of days. To be honest, I think it was like water off a duck's back!"

Liz's phone rang, she took it hands free.

"Friday at three?" Liz protested. "That's two days away. What's he doing, hibernating?"

"Grant's in London until lunchtime Friday on business. His secretary says it's Friday at three or Monday."

"I was hoping for an early Friday finish, I have illicit plans, Shakti, dirty and definitely illicit. I suppose I'll have to take Friday, worse luck."

Shakti shrieked with excitement. "Your personal life's your own boss but I'm slowly turning a darker shade of green."

Ruth laughed too and stole a glance at Liz as she turned right onto the A61.

"Back in fifteen minutes. See if you can come up with anything on JC. And Shakti…"

"Boss?"

"Don't tell more than six people about my weekend." She hung up.

Ruth was still chuckling. "It'll be all over the station before we're back, you know that? Well, spill!"

"Sorry, It's been planned for weeks. See if you can wipe the grin off my face on Monday. Hopefully it'll be there for a week!" She turned to Ruth, lifted her eyebrows and then winked.

Ruth giggled with over excitement and accidentally dribbled saliva down her chin.

Liz smiled and turned to Ruth, "How many Tunnock's Wafers are sold every week? I thought six million."

Ruth just dribbled even more.

***

Cyril sat in Café Nero and looked across at the Cenotaph. People huddled under umbrellas; the lunchtime dash had started later owing to the wet weather. There were few tourists brave enough to queue at the famous Betty's tea room as the persistent rain seem to drive at right angles to the road and penetrate the glazed veranda. He focussed on the myriad concentric rings made by the droplets of rain. As the water collected at the gutter's edge, each ripple died away as quickly as it was formed, to be followed by a further fusillade. His mobile vibrated in his jacket pocket stirring him from the mesmeric sight.

"Cyril, it's Julie. You've not called."

"Sorry, work."

"I know, this call is too! The metal sample found on the tape that covered Valerie Atkins's eyes is about a hundred years old so your pin idea sounds probable. Can you get hold of one, one that you mentioned, Charlie somebody?"

"Charles Horner. I can't say when but probably. When for?"

"Today?" She heard his sharp intake of breath. "Joking, Cyril. Whenever's possible."

"I'll do what I can. What are you doing tonight?" Cyril enquired hoping to add something positive to his schedule.

"Nothing, what's on offer?"

"Dinner at mine? Hopefully I'll have what you're searching for."

"What about the hat pin?" She giggled.

"Tonight at mine, beans and a couple of slices of toast!" Cyril hung up as a large smile spread across his lips.

Suddenly, the ambience in the café changed, it was as if someone had switched on a large light. The sun had broken cover from the grey banks of overcast cloud, rewarding the intrepid with a cracked scar of blue and a brilliant rainbow that contrasted sharply with the colours of the autumn day. He finished his coffee and left, walking swiftly to the rear of the War Memorial and onto James Street. Within two minutes he was on Albert Street.

The auctioneer's premises were tucked away in a row of shops. They were simply a large pair of black doors, no windows, just simple, large double doors. However, once inside it resembled the Tardis; the vast internal space seemed to defy its feeble façade. The entrance hall was brightly lit paintings to be sold in the next auction adorned the walls. Cyril took a moment to inspect them.

"Cyril Bennett you can neither afford them nor do you need any more!"

A middle-aged lady smiled at him whilst leaning through an opening at the top left of the corridor that served as a Reception.

"Wouldn't say no to that, Linda, nor the John Melville, but you're right about one thing, I can't afford them. Need more wall space too for that matter. Either that or sell some."

"Yes, I fancy the Melville, too. What can we do for you?"

"I'm interested in getting hold of a Charles Horner hatpin, to borrow. Any ideas?"

"None in this sale but I'll check the files to see if we have collectors on our books, maybe they'll lend you one. Have a look around and I'll find you."

Cyril wandered into the room opposite. He studied a Bronze of a seated female, all large thighs and legs.

"Hannah Frank, lovely. Glaswegian artist. Lived until she was a hundred. If you're lucky you might get it for a couple of grand," Linda commented.

Cyril whistled. "Any luck with the pin, Linda?"

She slipped a piece of paper into his hand. "Had a word with Mrs MacNamara, Ann MacNamara, lovely lady, collects all sorts and has a fantastic assortment of pins. I told her you were such a nice man so she's more than willing to loan one to you." She smiled, placing the details in Cyril's hand, holding on a little too long for comfort; it made him blush.

"I'm grateful. Good luck with the Melville." Cyril made a swift exit.

Once on the street, he glanced at the address. St Wilfred's Road. He would walk firstly crossing Stray Rein and then along the edge of The Stray. The sky had cleared considerably. It would also mean he could call at the supermarket on his return in preparation for his dinner date that evening.

St Wilfred's Road seemed to stretch forever. He checked the house number and glanced at the first house, relieved that the address for which he was searching was closer than he had imagined.

Cyril crunched his way down the gravel driveway. He again checked the address on the piece of paper just to be sure. Before he was half way down, he saw a face at the window. He raised his hand and smiled. The door was opened before he'd walked the rest of the way.

"Mr Bennett?" a lady of about eighty called.

Cyril nodded. "Mrs MacNamara, thanks very much for your help. I suppose it's not every day you get a request from someone to borrow a hat pin, especially from a male!"

"You'd be surprised these days. Please call me Ann."

Once inside Cyril was shown into the lounge. There were three hatpins positioned on the coffee table. Mahogany cabinets followed the room's periphery, each containing different collections of items. It more resembled a traditional museum than a lounge.

She noticed Cyril's eyes travel to each cabinet and smiled. "I just can't stop myself. Some folks are addicted to alcohol or drugs, with me its these things. I call them my tranklements. Can't resist a good auction. These three are all Charles Horner designed pins. I've taken the liberty of bringing three in different condition, basic, better and best. A bit like on Antiques Roadshow. I'm sure you watch it?"

"I'm one of those sad people, Ann, who has decided not to own a television set." Cyril did not give it his usual title of 'Idiot's Lantern', but the tone of his voice left her in no doubt as to the degree of enthusiasm he felt for the technology.

"I don't watch much to be honest, waste of time really, just the antique programmes and some soaps, the historical dramas are a favourite also..." She paused as if to take a breath. "University Challenge too, nearly forgot that one. Paxman is such a handsome man. Did I mention Top Gear? That's a particular weakness I just love fast cars and then there's…"

"May I?" Cyril needed to distract her to stop her non-stop chattering.

She nodded. "Please, help yourself."

Cyril picked up what he considered to be the basic pin. It was about five and a half inches in length topped with a round glass bead; the pin showed clear signs of age.

"What age are these?"

"They're all over a hundred years old. I think the one you're holding was made about 1905."

"Would it be possible to borrow all three? I'd need them for about two weeks. They'll be sent to Forensics, we need to do some comparative studies. I assure you they'll be well looked after and I'll return them personally."

"Please, happy to help our police." She smiled and left the room for a moment returning with three pin boxes. "It will be safer for the pins and yourself if you carry them in these."

Within half an hour Cyril had deposited the boxes at home and was at the supermarket. He had much to do.

***

Julie left the table holding a glass of red wine. "Not just a pretty face, Bennett. That cod loin was to die for."

Cyril smiled and removed the blue striped apron. "It was nothing, glad you enjoyed it," He put down his glass and collected the three boxes. "Here, another miracle. Who said men can't multi-task?"

Julie lifted the lid on the first box and removed the pin. "They're so fine. Certainly could be the weapon used. Can you leave them with me?"

"You've got a fortnight, no longer. Put them away… no shoptalk. Now what were you saying about my culinary skills?"

***

The small, black, plastic box lid was clearly marked:
Prometheus Hunting Pellets
100, cal. .22
Made in England

A gloved hand flicked the lid open and withdrew two of the pellets. Each pellet had a round, bullet-like metal nose behind which a plastic body wrapped a metal core. The plastic ensured a perfect calibre fit. Using a pair of long-nosed pliers, the first pellet was picked up by the bullet tip. The other hand held a pair of mole grips on the plastic. Carefully, one hand remained stationary whilst the grips were gently rotated. The metal element was easily removed leaving only the plastic sheath. This action was repeated four times. Two sheaths were needed but the grips could easily distort the integrity of the plastic. Each sheath was inspected and only two were chosen.

A bicycle spoke was clamped into a vice and sawn into two identical lengths. An end of one of the pieces was sharpened. Holding that piece of spoke in the vice, one of the plastic sheaths was slid five centimetres onto the shaft from the unsharpened end; the second was then threaded leaving a centimetre of metal showing. A small amount of fine superglue was applied; the final result resembled a tribal, hunting dart.

The remaining half of the spoke was put to one side; its rôle would be very different. The figure stretched, interlocking his fingers before bending them forcing the knuckles to crack. He admired the dart, running it through his fingers before collecting a break-barrel air rifle from the gun cabinet. He snapped the barrel open and inserted the dart. All was ready.

***

The farmyard was quiet. The cobbled square was still wet from the morning rain. A pungent odour lingered but those working there had become immune to the smell. Leaning on the far wall was a sheet of insulating board comprising thick, compressed foam. A small circle had been drawn as the target.

The rifle was lifted to the shoulder and the shooter focussed through the cylindrical gun sight positioned along the top of the gun. The sight was carefully adjusted until the centre of the target circle corresponded with the cross hairs of the sight. A finger curled onto the trigger. There was a slight popping sound as the finger squeezed and then silence. A millisecond later a puff of yellowy-white dust erupted from the board's surface as the dart buried itself deep into the soft, compacted foam. The dart had travelled forty yards and landed within the marked circle. A smile broke out on the shooter's face; it was accurate enough for the task ahead.

On inspection, the dart had penetrated the target leaving only the last quarter held in the foam. The rubber seals appeared intact. The rifle would not be fired again for three days. The dart and the other piece of spoke were placed in a box alongside the gun in the cabinet and the door was locked.

From an upstairs window, a solitary female had watched the test and had received a thumb's up. She turned to look at the large, muscular figure sitting at the table. His hands were spread flat out on the surface. Each nail on one hand was delicately painted a different colour. From between each finger, a gold chain ran to link with a bracelet that encircled his wrist. His feminine, homosexual persona was a disguise, a contradiction in visual terms that often proved to be a callous weapon. In many circles, Charles was known for his kindness and generosity but in others his reputation for cruelty, some might say pure evil, could not be underestimated; it would be a fool who judged this book by its cover. Both Coulson and Atkins would attest to that.

"That went better than we'd hoped." She crossed the room.

He looked up, there was no reaction. The eyes with which she made contact were cold.

"What we need now is to find Atkins's computer. If it had been located already this place would have been swarming with police. It's still out there. I'm overdue some remedial therapy at home."

Suddenly there was a pause and a smile spread across his sunburned face. With an almost effeminate lisp he spoke again, his tone was exaggeratedly camp.

"The Mediterranean is so kind to my old bones at this time of year, whereas Yorkshire can be so cruel. Like the birds, darling, I need to fly!" He brought his hands up to his sides and flapped them gently. "Speaking of migratory birds, the new consignment is here and the farm is really efficient. I'd hate for us to close it down owing to the cuckoo we think is crowding the nest; cuckoos take so much feeding at the expense of everyone else, they simply have to be removed!"

He returned his palms to the table and his facial expression changed yet again.

"There were four illegals brought from the coast, this time at some considerable risk, it's getting more and more difficult with Calais as it is. It used to be so civilized and now it's just a bloody bun fight. Making fewer runs comprising fewer selected passengers is the only way to proceed in today's climate and that makes me so cross."

Christina noted a real anger but failed to heed her observation before opening her mouth.

"You're not here just because of the internet creep or the possible fear of what that girl might report, that was already in hand, they'd have just disappeared. Isn't this arsing about with spokes a little too theatrical, Charles?"

It was a brave thing to say and as soon as she had said it she knew from the expression on Charles' face that she had just crossed an invisible line. His demeanour changed as quickly as a heartbeat.

"There's more to this than what we have today, more than all of this." He spread his hands as if encompassing the room and the surroundings. "Do you know how long I've worked in moving people and drugs? No you fucking don't. Do you know how many times I've been caught and punished? No you fucking don't. Do you know how many people I've killed with these?"

He brought his hands together and held them out open-palmed. "No you fucking don't but if you talk to me again like that I can assure you that there'll be one more stain on them. My being here is not only professional but also very personal. I'm chasing a man and we go back a long way."

He paused. Christina felt the venom radiate across the table as his hands clenched into fists. Unconsciously, she took a step backwards.

"He's one interfering bastard who split my fine-tuned, inner circle of friends asunder, a circle which worked successfully for years and then he comes along… It would be so marvellous to strike and run, to be a shadow of the Grim Reaper and remove only his arrogant self-confidence. I plan to make the shit pay in guilt and I plan to make him live with the torment that guilt brings. I'll make him realise that sometimes you can't help those who most need it. I'll crush him, crush him mentally. As time allows the guilt to fester, it will render him human waste and you'll help me achieve that!"

He lifted his eyes and stared at Christina. "I want the computers and I want the cuckoo but you know that already, bitch. Think on, I also want Bennett."

Christina leaned against the wall trying to compose herself. She moved her hands behind her in an endeavour to keep them from shaking before she summoned the courage to speak.

"I'm sorry, Charles, please forgive me. We've people, shall we say, visiting the friends we found in Valerie Atkins's address book on her phone. There's nothing showing on her texts and she was very tidy with her emails. It'll take time. Coulson made a classic error, it took just one slip. We knew it would happen eventually and that we'd locate him sooner or later. He just got too cocky, the bastard. The good thing was that finding him led us to locate Atkins. Letting him continue with his computer venom for a while enabled us to work on her, but we still can't find the Judas figure, the one giving away our sensitive details, but we'll find him." She walked back to the window. "Besides, discovering

Atkins's different appetites was a bonus. We couldn't get rid of her until we'd destroyed Coulson; you did that so well."

Her obsequious tone could have ignited more of his wrath but Charles's expression had changed. He smiled and admired his fingernails. He suddenly recalled her earlier remark. "The videos were so theatrical and a real pleasure to watch. I just loved the masks… kinky… and as you all know, I adore kinky."

Christina was quick to see the pointed comment and moved towards him. It was now time to be placatory and more submissive, to play the game, as the term cuckoo clouded her mind.

"I do listen… It's all about patience, Charles, as you so often say. It's all about waiting for the correct moment. The fear was that Coulson would go public as soon as he had anything concrete. He was close, especially when he became involved with Atkins."

Christina Cameron's phone rang. Charles looked up and frowned.

"It can only be the auction house." She put her finger to her lips.

"Hello."

She nodded.

"Yes, Sylvia Bentham speaking. Thank you for getting back to me. Did you like the painting?... Good, good… so much? Why that's more than Mr Crompton thought… yes, in the same auction if you would. Call me on this number? No, sorry I'm changing my phone contract so I'll ring you with the new contact number and address before the auction if that's all right… Good. Thanks for your trouble."

Christina removed the SIM card from the phone. "Once they've sold your murder weapons, they will no longer be a worry." She checked her watch. "I need to get back."

Charles simply smiled holding, out his hand.

"We have more from your Charles Horner collection I take it?" He emphasised the word 'Charles'. "I doubt Bennett will see the connection until it's all too late but we have to give him a sporting chance."

Christina nodded and then passed him the SIM card. He put it in his mouth and swallowed it. "A boyfriend of mine should possibly be able to make a trunk call with that later." He giggled as he left the room. For a big man he made mincing look so easy. Frightening, but easy.

Chapter Eleven

The dark blue Range Rover pulled up on Giles Street, Netherthong. It was 18:20 and already dark. The stone-built block of apartments resembled a small woollen mill situated in the heart of the village. The vehicle passed through the archway and was parked in one of the bays marked 'Private'.

"Number 13. Lucky for some but somehow I doubt it will be us today!" the driver called cheerily as he climbed from the vehicle.

Karen Johnson opened the door keeping the security chain attached.

"DS Sharples and this is DC Flint. Sorry to bother you but it's about Valerie Atkins. Our colleagues in North Yorkshire Police have asked us to just clarify a few points from their meeting with you." He held out a fake warrant card and smiled. "Nights are drawing in too quickly for my liking." He flashed another smile and looked at his colleague, before swiftly hiding the fake ID.

"It'll only take a couple of minutes," she said and smiled too.

Karen slid the chain and opened the door. "I'm expecting my partner home any time now. A few minutes you say?"

"When you were with Valerie on the weekend in Harrogate did she have her phone, iPad and computer with her?"

"She had her phone and may well have had her iPad in her bag, it's only the smaller one; as for her laptop definitely not. I can only confirm the phone."

"Could it have been in her hotel room? I believe you stayed over at..." he paused.

"The Croft."

"Yes, thanks. I had it written here somewhere, forgive me."

"Maybe. I shared with Sheila Walsh. Nancy Anders and Gail Gough were in the other room. Val had her own so she could have. Couldn't say for certain."

"We believe that the contents of her computers may hold the key as to why she died, but so far we've, or should I say our North Yorkshire colleagues, have yet to locate them. You spoke with whom at Harrogate?"

Karen frowned at the question. "Graydon, yes a Detective Graydon."

DC Flint smiled. "Worked under her when she was in Merseyside Police."

A key was inserted into the lock. Karen smiled. "It'll be Dan. He's usually home earlier but they had a computer problem, strangely enough."

Dan was a little taken aback when he saw the two strangers.

"It's the police about Val, they're just leaving."

Dan looked at them both and stood to one side to allow them to leave.

"Wondered who'd parked in my space. Pity you didn't read 'Private Parking'. Big letters too, not hard to see."

"Sorry, we thought we'd be only a few minutes. Our apologies. Thanks for your time."

He kicked the door closed behind them. "What the bloody hell did they want?"

"Val's computers. They were sent to see me by Harrogate Police. They think that something stored on one of Val's computers is the reason she was killed."

Dan frowned. He put a hand on each of her shoulders. "You've been interviewed before, did they ask you about them then?"

"Think so, Christ it's been so upsetting I can't truly recall. Can we go to the pub for a drink, maybe something to eat? I just need to go out. Dan they didn't know anything from the interview, they didn't know the hotel and they asked who'd interviewed me. It just didn't feel right. What could be on her computer to make someone kill her?"

Dan held back the surge of panic and forced a smile before wrapping his arms around her. "You know how busy coppers are today, Christ, most don't know if it's Easter or Pentecost! Pub sounds good. I need a shower."

He disappeared into the bedroom and looked for Karen's bag. He took out her purse and found the card she'd been given by Harrogate Police. He dialled the mobile number.

"DS Graydon." Liz was just clearing her desk; it had been a long day.

"Hi, my name's Dan Rowney, I'm Karen Johnson's partner. You interviewed her about Valerie Atkins's murder."

"Yes, has she remembered something else? She's all right isn't she?"

"Yes, yes. Have you requested that the police call and ask more questions? We've just had a visit and I'm uncomfortable with that. No pre call, they just turned up at the apartment."

"Not that I'm aware. Give me a second." Liz brought up the case notes on screen and checked to see if any requests for county force co-operation had been requested. There was nothing. "Why are you suspicious, Dan?" She double-checked the file whilst she was speaking.

"They, a male and a female, arrived in a blue Range Rover but I've never seen a plain police car with a tow-bar and a GB sticker unless you're using your own vehicles now!"

"The cuts haven't gone that far I'm pleased to say. That's observant. I don't suppose you got the number?"

"Indeed, it was parked in my allocated space. They couldn't read either!"

Liz smiled. "Leave it with me. Ask Karen to make a note of all that they asked and if you can, jot down a description of them both. I'll get someone round within the hour. When they arrive they'll use the words *Spa Town* that's so you know they are legit. Give them all the details you can. I'll chase this registration and be in touch."

Liz checked the numbers for Val's friends who had attended the reunion weekend and dialled each one. Both Nancy Anders and Gail Gough had received visits from the police regarding the whereabouts of Valerie's computers. They each gave a brief description of the officers and in both cases they appeared to be the same, a male and female officer. She dialled Sheila Walsh's mobile. There was no answer.

An email appeared on her desktop screen. The registration plate should be presumed to be cloned with further checks in progress. The car was registered to a farmer in Scotland. Within minutes, Liz had requested that South Yorkshire Police put an immediate watch on Sheila Walsh's home. Liz had given details of the vehicle and liaised with West Yorkshire for them to forward descriptions of the people impersonating officers as soon as they had the information. She had also tried to activate a watch on ANPR (Automatic Number Plate Recognition) but it had already been done. She relaxed a little, stretching her legs under the desk, trying to push blood into her toes; her feet were numb. She checked her watch.

Within twenty-minutes she had received a full description of the impersonating officers and confirmation that West Yorkshire were liaising with South Yorkshire. It was now a waiting game. There was a likelihood that they would not approach Walsh on the same day but there was no guarantee. She added all the notes to file, uploaded and decided to head home.

***

Karen and Dan had given as much information as possible and the officers left full of assurances that they should not be contacted again. Another two word code was given to ensure that if they were, then they would know if it were legitimate.

"I'm pissed off and bloody famished! Come on, the pub calls," Dan moaned taking a deep breath.

Karen smiled. "My hero." She leaned over and kissed him. "Why would anyone be murdered for things stored on a computer, why?"

Dan held her coat. He didn't have the heart to tell her. Besides Valerie had sworn him to secrecy when she had handed him the computers. She had called him that day and asked him to drop Karen off and then wait for her in Princess Square; she had something for him. It all seemed very dramatic. *Keep them at work with all the others you look after. What's on these is my future. I'm going to be back where I was, Dan, you just wait and see.* He remembered that she had seemed so nervous, had kept looking around as she handed the plastic carrier bag through the passenger window, yet also so excited. *You must promise me to tell no one, definitely not Karen if you love her. It'll be all right; I'll be safe once it's out there but until then…* He recalled that she had winked at him and smiled. He had laughed, thinking she might already be a little drunk and would be calling him on Monday to ask for some repair work or virus removal. That was her usual style but he had been so wrong.

With her death and after the visit, Dan's curiosity had started to gnaw away and expose a cruel fear. Whatever was stored was obviously dangerous and the last thing he wanted right now was to put Karen in harm's way.

"Thought you were famished, Dan Rowney. I'm standing here like cheese at tuppence and you're in a daydream. Anyhow, clever clogs, what is the difference between Easter and Pentecost?"

Dan laughed for the first time since arriving home. "Seven weeks." He collected the keys and they left the flat.

***

The blue Range Rover had shed the cloned plates, peeled from the originals beneath. The vehicle headed away from Netherthong before turning left up Thick Hollins Road. The destination was Denshaw and then the M62. They were professional and covered their tracks well, nothing was taken for granted so they stuck to the speed limits.

"Make a crap copper, me. My eyes were all over the place and all over her. Christ I could've given her one there and then! Tasty. Wonder if she liked to party like her bloody mate, sex-ee Valer-eee." He exaggerated the end of each word so as to form a lascivious grin before allowing his tongue to flash in and out of his mouth. "Could see her on a video spread across that bloody table with me behind her." He took one hand off the wheel and grabbed his crotch. "Dan wouldn't be in the fucking equation then I can tell you that for sure. Charles would like to watch that too."

"He's more interested in you than her! I'm as safe as houses but he still bloody terrifies me that man. He's like a bloody chameleon; one minute he's as hard as bloody nails, testosterone flying everywhere and then he turns down his wrist, his voice moves up an octave and he's everyone's favourite queer."

"Makes out he wouldn't swat a fly."

"My arse! Christ, he's one evil bastard. When's he going back?"

"When we clean this mess up. If we don't it'll mean a full close down and I mean full. You can well imagine what that would mean. No witnesses." He moved his hand from his crotch and ran a finger across his throat. "I've heard dreadful things! He came in supporting a new shipment; with all the migrants in Europe, times are difficult. He comes, checks all's well, cleans up if needs be and then buggers off. His place in the south of France is supposed to be magnificent, all pink and white, if the rumours are correct. Some even say that he has pink, stone lions on each of the gate posts!"

Chapter Twelve

Friday morning broke with a clear blue sky only marred by what might be interpreted as a shepherd's warning; streaks of orange edged with vermillion crazed the lower horizon, allowing shafts of sunlight to break like ethereal search lights into the blue. A light mist clung to the trees of The Stray bringing an edge to the autumnal day.

Dan Rowney was at work early. He had, with a degree of reluctance, retrieved Valerie's laptop and iPad from the IT secure store. He lifted the lid and pressed the start button. Within seconds it demanded a password. Dan had set up a Dashlane Password Manager over twelve months ago at Valerie's request, naming himself as her emergency contact. He was relieved to see that it had not been changed; he now had emergency access to her data.

He opened his own Mac before quickly requesting the access to Valerie's data. It would take four days, the time he had set for her to be able to stop any emergency request should she ever need to. Knowing the circumstances, he knew that would not be the case. He then picked up his phone.

***

Liz Graydon had noticed the red sky and hoped that it was not a harbinger of disaster. The plume of smoke silently rising from the machine had made her curse. She pushed the metal knife deep into the bowels of the toaster more like a mechanic than a surgeon, twisting it and prodding in an attempt to extract the over-enthusiastically charred piece of sliced bread. The acrid smell filled her nostrils and the kitchen as her expletives were accompanied by the scream of a smoke alarm.

"Shit! Shit! Shit!"

She then realised that she had not unplugged the toaster!

She had clothes hanging from various door casings ready to be chosen and then packed for her weekend away. Now, she would likely turn up smelling of a burnt offering. It was the phone dancing along the work surface that caught her eye before she made out the ring tone drowned by the alarm.

"Fuck!"

"Graydon!"

Dan was rather taken aback by the almost hostile response and the sound of the alarm in the background.

"Hold a minute." Liz stood on a chair and silenced the alarm, took a deep breath and tried to calm herself. "Sorry, a bit of a domestic issue with some toast but the situation's now under control."

"Is that DS Graydon?" Dan's voice came over as uncertain.

"Yes. To whom am I speaking?"

"Sergeant, it's Dan Rowney, Karen Johnson's partner. We spoke last night."

Liz tensed. "Have they been back?"

"No, no but I need to speak with you. I have Valerie's computers, well laptop and pad. They are password secure but I'm the emergency account holder."

"Where are they?"

Dan explained the whole story and assured her that they were held in a secure IT area, but the sooner he could hand them over the more comfortable he would feel. Liz also wanted to get her hands on them too and she arranged to meet him at his place of work. After she had hung up she called Cyril who was seemingly having his normal, organised morning routine. She was instructed to meet with Dan as soon as possible.

She quickly packed her overnight case and returned the other items of clothing to her wardrobe. Breakfast was now forgotten, but the smell of burning still lingered, killing her appetite. Once her bag was in the hall she smiled. "Let's just get this day over with and..." She didn't finish the sentence, her ring tone interrupted.

"It's Cyril. Are you there yet? I've cleared it with West Yorkshire."

"I'm going to Huddersfield, not this side of Leeds! I'll ring when I'm there."

"Liz, get all the details, major password and log in details. Take care."

She set the Sat Nav. to take her via the A61, M62. It showed a travel time of eighty minutes. At least now she could relax.

***

When Liz entered, Dan Rowney was waiting in the entrance of Priorspur Electronics, a converted woollen mill that was both modern and light. Although they had never met, Dan instinctively knew that she was police.

Liz walked towards the Reception desk.

"DS Graydon?"

She nodded and approached Dan. She noticed that he carried a laptop case. He held out his hand.

"Thanks for coming so soon. It's here and to be honest it frightens me. Since her death, I've been reluctant to let anyone know about the arrangement. Before her death I just thought that she was after some free IT support; that was Valerie all over! My only worry is that I'm the key, I hold the password and whoever killed Val for what's in here." He lifted the case. "Then I or Karen could be next."

"The sooner we find what's locked in her data, the safer you'll be. Once it's in our hands we can act. For them it's over. Why can't we access it immediately?"

"It's the way it works, I set a time lock to protect Val. You'll only be able to access the data after four days, that's Monday morning at about seven. I've written down the procedure but your guys will have no trouble. The master password is here."

Dan handed her an envelope. "Without this, nobody would be able to retrieve the data. If you lose that and anything happens to me it's lost forever."

Liz thought that he sounded very melodramatic and took the envelope, sliding it into her inside pocket. She wanted to say, *Don't die until Monday,* before adding a big smile but she could sense the stress Dan was under. She held out her hand for the case.

"I'll certainly be pleased to see the back of that, believe me!"

Liz could see the pressure lift as he released the case into her care.

"Nothing personal but let's hope that this is the last time we'll meet. You've got my number if I can be of assistance but I've made the procedure all so very clear in the note I've put in the envelope."

Within minutes Liz was pulling out of the car park, the bag safely locked in the boot. She rang Cyril.

"Bennett."

"All done. Do you want this taking directly to Newby Wiske? It can't be accessed until Monday at the earliest?"

"Yes, please. I'll let them know you're on your way. See you back here."

***

Liz turned off the road towards the gates of Newby Wiske, a large seventeenth century hall set in thirty-five acres of grounds. It had been the headquarters of the North Yorkshire Police for forty years. Although a beautiful building, it was expensive to maintain and the facilities were getting past their sell by date. The facility was no longer able to support efficiently the demands of a modern police service. She would be sad to see it go; already an alternative in Northallerton had been allocated. The concave hedge seemed almost to suck you past the lodge as you drove in from the road. Liz glanced at the 'For Sale' sign. *No doubt it will be converted into a hotel in a couple of years' time*, she thought. Within minutes she had deposited the laptop with a Digital Forensic Technician before heading back to Harrogate.

***

A coffee in one hand, Liz threw on her ID and made her way to the Incident Room. Owen was sitting staring at the boards and making the occasional note. He turned as she entered before checking his watch.

"Good of you to join us. Late start, early finish is it? Believe you're away for a weekend of carnal exploitation?" He raised his eyebrows and smiled. "I'm jealous."

"Late, Christ it's been a catalogue of bloody errors and you're not improving my day. Can't get my head straight. Who told you, anyway?"

"Lips are sealed."

"Valerie's computers are with the techy boys and girls but…" She interrupted herself as her hand felt the edge of the envelope tucked inside her jacket pocket. "Shit! Bloody burnt toast, alarm, smoky clothes, Huddersfield, Newby Wiske and now this!" She threw it onto the table.

Owen leaned over and picked it up. "Love letter? French letter for the weekend?"

She snatched it back with one hand and slapped his head with the other before explaining the true course of her morning. Owen listened.

***

Cyril Bennett had just finished briefing his Chief Constable who seemed happy with the progress made on the double murders, especially the acquisition of the missing computer. He smiled to himself as he thought of the Chief standing behind a desk piled high with papers and pebbles; his desk always reminded Cyril of the north face of the Eiger. He returned the phone and then picked up a note left by DC Smirthwaite.

HOLMES link: Dark Range Rover reported collecting person or persons in what appeared to be a rendezvous at Flixton. One other vehicle involved. No numbers identified. Rover last seen heading away from the coast towards Malton on the A64. Possible migrant transfer.

This would be the fifth recorded incident of migrant activity over a fourteen-month period in that area but the only one referencing a dark coloured Range Rover.

The smuggling of migrants was becoming popular with the criminal fraternity, providing easy money for a task that used to present few risks. Often linked with the shipping of drugs, it made for a lucrative trade. Cyril had heard that those being shipped to Greece from Turkey were dumping life vests partly made up of waterproof containers filled with cocaine. The dealers were clearing them from the beaches before stripping the drugs and moving the contraband inland. If seventy per cent of the drugs were recovered then it was a financial win-win.

Cyril noted the light drain from the room. He turned to see Owen.

"Liz is back. The guy who had Valerie's lap top is a little anxious."

"We have the master password and details?"

Owen nodded.

"Then he's nothing to worry about. I take it he's activated the emergency request?"

Owen nodded again. "We just have to make sure we're the only recipients of the data. Shouldn't we be keeping a watch on him until Monday? It wouldn't take much to get the info from him, especially if they decide to get rough and hold his partner. Just thinking out loud!"

Cyril drummed his fingers on the table, weighing up the risk against the cost; costing was a growing priority and a major consideration no matter how sensitive the policing. "Contact West Yorks and call in a favour. Get Liz to ring…" Cyril seemed stuck for a name.

"Dan Rowney." Owen offered.

"Yes, Rowney, thanks. Once you have the go ahead, let them know what's happening. After Monday they'll be safe anyway." Cyril drew on his electronic cigarette. "And Owen…"

Owen returned.

"Thanks!"

***

Liz had not really been able to settle all day. It was the traumatic start; after all, she had played cook, fireman, agony aunt, and courier within the course of a few hours. More to the point, it was likely that her blissful anticipation of the weekend ahead that was the catalyst for her anxiety. She checked her watch for the fourth time within the hour, how slowly the hands seemed to be turning!

Shakti observed, "A watched pot never boils, Boss. That's the fifth time you've looked at your watch in the last hour. What time is your appointment this afternoon? More importantly, what's his name? Is he tall, handsome with a large…" She paused and batted her eyelashes. "Large, thick, wallet?" She smiled and assumed a look of total innocence.

Liz put her finger to her lips and ran it across them. "From now, Shakti Misra, my lips are well and truly sealed."

She removed the envelope from her pocket and made one more call to the technician's at Newby Wiske. It was full of apologies, thanks and promises.

"Yes, email… Yes, Michael, right now. No, no errors, I know I should have left it. I'll even photograph it and mail it just to make sure, promise!"

She turned to the keyboard and started typing the information that Dan had placed in the envelope.

"Shakti, please check this. I'm all bloody fingers and thumbs!"

"Your date won't be too pleased to hear that! Yep, exactly right. Now you can relax."

She took the photograph and mailed it directly to Michael.

Liz checked her watch again and shook it. "Bloody hell, getting as bad as Flash Bennett, bless him. If I drive slowly I'll not be early and then…" She smiled.

"Don't forget briefing at 07:00 Monday sharp. Bright eyed and bushy tailed."

Liz just pretended to yawn, stretched, then left.

***

Liz parked the car outside the Stray Agency it was 14:48. Although the sky was the colour of elephant hide, there was no rain. She was eager to get this interview over with and head home. Her overnight case was already packed. She was due to catch a train to Leeds at 19:05. Even now, she felt a frisson as her nerves combined with the feeling of utter excitement crashing in the pit of her stomach. She dropped the sun visor and stared at the vanity mirror before straightening her hair. She took a deep breath and left the car. Her phone rang.

"Graydon."

"How you feeling, Boss? Just wanted to wish you a happy weekend!"

"Thanks Shakti and thanks for the present. Strawberry flavour is just me! This phone will be off in twenty minutes so please tell your six friends." She could hear Shakti and Owen giggle as she hung up. It made her relax a little.

Liz turned her phone to silent and smiled. She counted her blessings that she had come to Harrogate. Cyril Bennett was a delight to work with, a bit old fashioned and a little too proper at times, but she would not swap him and the team was just that, a team. *Strawberry indeed!* she thought. *I don't think so!*

She climbed the three steps that led to the large, Victorian door. She too noticed the unpolished brass plaque. A lamp was lit prematurely above the arched doorway. She pressed the intercom. A garbled message dragged its way from the speaker.

"DS Liz Graydon to see Mr Grant. I have an appointment at three."

There was a buzz and then a click as the door sprung free from the lock. Liz pushed and entered the hall. Christina Cameron was standing at the far end by the stairs. She was petite and slim. She smiled at Liz.

"This way, please. Mr Grant should be here any moment."

Liz was shown into a large, elegant room. Two red leather settees were positioned centrally and on either side of the fireplace. The walls were covered with photographs, one of which she noticed was Valerie. One wall featured a large painting hanging centrally but at a slight angle. Liz stood before it and studied the quaint industrial image before straightening it. She stood back to check it was straight; she had a hatred of crooked pictures as well as crooked people. The depicted figures, almost cartoon-like, were heading to the factory gates. Children were climbing walls. The red terraced houses contrasted with the pink and white of the smoke-laden sky as if contradicting the smoking chimneys. It had an almost comic quality that brought a smile to her face. She looked in the bottom left hand corner of the painting and read the signature, *G W Birks 69*. For a moment her butterflies had gone. She checked her watch whilst growing increasingly annoyed. Grant was late. She decided to give him five more minutes.

At 15:12 she stood and went to the door only to be intercepted by his secretary.

"I'm sorry he's running late, it's not like him," protested Christina, whilst emphasising the fact with a facial expression that clearly showed her annoyance. She shook her head. "Sorry! It's not like Mr Grant to leave anyone waiting and certainly not the police."

"I have another more pressing appointment so I'll have to go. Please tell Mr Grant that I'll call on Monday." Liz pressed the door release and descended the steps. As she approached her car she heard a phone ring in a distant office.

Liz opened her car door, climbed in and smiled to herself before removing her phone. She dialled Shakti's mobile.

"It's Liz, there is a God after all. Grant's been delayed coming back from London so an early finish for me. Strawberry indeed! Just thought I'd let you know that in half an hour I'll be soaking in a hot bath of sweet smelling bubbles in preparation for..." She hung up.

It was then that she noticed Christina Cameron waving from the doorway before making her way quickly to the car. Liz opened the window.

"Mr Grant's phoned, there was a slight delay with his train. He'll be five minutes at the most he's assured me and he's asked if you could kindly wait."

Liz sighed, checked her watch and opened the car door.

"Come on, I'll get you a coffee. Sorry to mess you about."

Liz sat and looked at the painting again as Christina brought in the coffee.

"For some reason I just love the naivety of that painting." Liz pointed.

"The Birks? He's a Leeds' artist, used to be a window dresser can you believe. I bought it at a local auction. Too big for my apartment but I love it. Mr Grant was kind enough to let me hang it here. I often have my lunch where you're sitting and I just stare at it; you see something different every time." She smiled and turned to the painting.

Liz put her coat and bag onto a chair and picked up the coffee. She sipped cautiously but it was cool and so she drank more quickly. She didn't finish it. A fuzzy haze seemed to fill her head as if she were drifting. She wondered if she had overdone her anticipation of the weekend ahead but then she began to feel as though she were floating. Suddenly she felt scared and nauseous; she quickly realised what was happening to her. She tried to lift the coffee cup to her nose to smell it but Ketamine is odourless and without taste. The cup fell from her fingers before breaking into fragments that scattered across the polished wooden floor. A trace of saliva dribbled uncontrollably from the side of her mouth as she tried to focus on the figure standing before her. All she saw was her own right arm being extended and her sleeve being rolled back. She neither felt the needle nor heard Christina telling her that all would be well. Liz felt as though she were elsewhere, she was totally oblivious to her surroundings. She now neither felt nor cared about the arms that held her and the eagerly anticipated weekend ahead never entered her drug-addled brain.

Christina slipped on a pair of skin-coloured protective gloves and took the phone from Liz's bag. She held the phone's circular pad to Liz's limp index finger in the hope that she added finger print acceptance. The screen lit. She then looked at the text messages. Keep her still, only her fingers are to touch this screen. She read them through.

"Bloody hell, she's got a dirty weekend planned. Train to Leeds tonight. Someone called Jim. Lucky Jim! I think not!" Christina slid Liz's paralysed finger down the screen and began to type a message with it. Christina had noticed that Liz always signed off her message to him with the name 'Pook', ending with four 'kisses'. She followed suit.

'Jim, something serious has cropped up at work and I can't make it this weekend, sooooo sorry. I'll make it up to you. It'll be worth the wait, believe me! Don't call me before Monday. You know the work I do. Just think about what's waiting. When you get this show you love me and understand by sending just a kiss. Pook xxxx.'

She turned the phone off silent before looking at the man holding Liz. The phone made a sound like an old claxon. A single cross filled the space on the screen.

"Technology's, wonderful!" Christina whispered into Liz's now deaf ear.

Christina put on Liz's coat; it was a little on the small size but if anyone noticed her entering the flat, it would be a useful disguise. She picked up Liz's bag, opened it and checked inside to ensure that Liz's keys were there. She added the phone.

"You know where to take her."

Christina left through the front door.

It had not been difficult finding the apartment. She had followed Liz twice to ensure that she had the correct home address, the third time she had checked the name on the pigeonhole post box in the entrance hall. Within ten minutes she was pulling up outside Liz's apartment. She parked the car, slid on some dark, protective overshoes, locked the vehicle and entered through the main door. Liz's flat was on the second floor. Quickly she looked at the post boxes fixed to the left wall. Without touching them, she ran her finger down stopping at each name until she reached *E Graydon.* She inserted a key from the bunch and opened the small door; four letters had been posted. She collected them before depositing the piece of bicycle spoke, onto which had been added a paper tag simply containing one sentence: K□NI-MAN DAI, K□NI-MAN BεR AM. She raised her shoulders and smiled as the letterbox door was closed and locked. She then took the stairs to the second floor.

It was a gamble, but Christina presumed that, owing to the age of the building, there would be no alarm. She held her breath as she slipped the key into the lock. It wouldn't turn. She looked carefully at the three other keys on the ring. Using the second key, she pushed the door ajar. Before entering she paused and held her breath, waiting for the warning bleep indicating that an alarm needed a code. To her relief, there was only silence. She pushed the door open.

Once inside, she closed the door and located the light switch. An overnight case sat to the left of the hall. Taking off Liz's coat, she dropped it carefully onto the case before putting the phone, the retrieved mail and the keys on the small side table. She glanced around a second time and it was then that she saw the corner of the envelope protruding from Liz's inner coat pocket. She opened it and read the details. She read it again. A flush of excitement made her tingle and utter a single question. "Why?" She returned it to the coat pocket, making one final visual check before turning and switching off the light. She dropped the latch on leaving. It was done. As the door closed behind her she paused. Voices could be heard drifting up from the entrance hall at the bottom of the stairs. Christina looked at the coverings on her shoes; should she remove them in case they were heading to the second flat on this floor, keep them on and just leave the building, or wait? The consequences of each action instantly flashed through her mind and she decided on the latter option. She controlled her breathing. Her sense of hearing seemed to be heightened. The phantom voices were now laughing and then she heard a door close, the sounds slowly evaporating. Relieved, she moved to the top of the stairs before cautiously descending. The entrance hall was empty. Sweat dribbled down the inner parts of her arms.

Once outside, the cold air hit her like a slap, it seemed so bracing. She took a deep breath before moving down the drive and onto the street. The streetlights had just come on, offering a dull, pink glow, a complement to the autumnal dusk's misty light. After two hundred yards she removed the overshoes and headed back to the office. If everything went to plan, at worst they would have twenty-four hours but at best it would be Monday morning before anyone knew that Liz Graydon was missing. It had been easier than she could possibly have imagined.

***

Owen received a call from West Yorkshire Police. Dan Rowney had apparently left work early on account of a phone call from his partner. The secretary mentioned that she had an emergency. They had checked their apartment but it was empty. Dan's car wasn't there either. Checks of local hospitals had proved negative and both their mobiles were off. A neighbour intimated that Karen had left the building in the company of a man at about 13:30. She looked anxious, but that was all she could reveal. Owen took Dan's work number and requested that someone remain at the apartment block in case they returned.

He rang Liz but her phone went directly to answer phone. "Shit!"

Owen found Shakti at a desk in the Incident Room. "Did Liz contact Dan Rowney before she left, do you know? Can't raise her!"

"Remember, she had a meeting with Grant, Valerie's agent at three but he didn't show." She looked at the time on the computer screen. "About now, she'll be dossing in a bath full of bubbles, early finish, said she'd be turning her phone off. You were here when she called, when I spoke with her, remember." Shakti checked the computer to see what Liz had uplifted, but there was no record of when she had logged on. She crossed to the desk Liz was using before flicking through her notes. "Nothing here also, why?"

"We're arranging police support for Dan and his partner for the weekend owing to the sensitivity of the data he's party to but it appears they've both gone AWOL. He left work after receiving some kind of emergency call from his partner, Karen Johnson. There's no sign of either of them nor of his car. She was last seen accompanied by a stranger. That's it. An alert is out for them and his vehicle."

Owen picked up the phone and waited. He looked at Shakti and raised his eyebrows. "I don't want button one or pigging two, I want a real bloody person for Christ sa… Hello DS Owen from North Yorkshire Police, I should like to speak to someone who saw Dan Rowney leave the premises today, it's a matter of urgency."

He listened as the Receptionist repeated what she had told the police when they had called at the office earlier. Owen went cold for a moment and interrupted.

"Did the police come for Mr Rowney or did they arrive after he left?"

"It was a good hour after Mr Rowney left when they called. Dan drove off like the devil was after him, Dan Rowney, that is. Not the way to treat a company car in my opinion, all smoking tyres. Is he in trouble?"

"What did he say as he left?"

"He tossed over his ID in a bit of a panic, suggesting that there was some domestic emergency. That's all. Logged him out at…. 13:47."

"Was he carrying anything?"

"Mr Owen, Mr Rowney goes nowhere without his laptop, he's our best IT guy. We call him the PC Doctor, even wears a white coat! I'm sure he'll find a way to take it to his grave."

Owen wondered just how appropriate that statement might be, but said nothing. Thanking the Receptionist he noted her name and direct number.

"Wherever he's gone he has his laptop with him."

Owen's mobile rang, it was control. West Yorks had located Dan's car. He looked at Shakti and mouthed what he was hearing. "Are Forensics on the way? Please ask them to keep us informed."

"No sign of him?"

"Nothing, we were too bloody late. Keep trying Liz."

"Sir, she's away for the weekend. She only collected the computer and delivered it. She sent the master password and an image of it to the Tech people. I checked it for her. See!" She located the relevant file. "Here! We have all that we need, Liz doesn't need to be here."

Owen just grunted and left to find Cyril.

"You're blocking the light, either move away from the door and sit down or communicate and go."

"No sign of either Rowney or his partner. Car's be found abandoned on Wassenden Head Road between Meltham and…"

Owen didn't finish as he noted Cyril's expression, one that said do not tell me the bleeding obvious!

"Any road, Sir. No sign of the driver."

"The Moors' murderers, Owen. You studied the case at police training? Please say that you did."

Owen nodded. "Some kids, five I think, some never found. Brady and Hindley buried them out on the moorlands not far from Manchester. One's still inside."

"Same piece of moorland the car was found. Can be bleak in the winter, cut by the Pennine Way. Why there? Could they have asked him to meet? Has he gone home and found a note? Forensics?"

"On their way. Where have I heard the word Hindley recently?" Owen pulled a face, screwing his eyes as if in deep thought.

"You'll rupture something, Owen, if you're not careful!"

"That's it!' Owen clicked his finger and thumb as his facial gurn evaporated. "Valerie's brother, that's it. He buggered off after having a tiff with Val's partner to a place called Hindley Green. Teaching job. Thought I'd heard it recently."

"Remind me, Owen. Hindley Green is where?"

Owen nearly fell off his chair. For the first time in all the years they had been together, his boss's geographical knowledge had deserted him.

"Hindley Green it's near Wigan."

"Yes, yes, between Hindley and Leigh. How could I possibly forget?"

Owen frowned, sure that Cyril had known all along.

"Hindley... Coincidence, that's all. Get onto the National ANPR Data centre for any references to Range Rovers within the last four hours in a twenty mile radius of where the car was left. For the sake of our sanity, get them to narrow it down to those painted in dark colours. Where's Liz?"

"Off early, social weekend." Owen winked at Cyril.

"Weekend, Owen? What on earth is that? Social weekend... never heard of it. Go for your weekend after you've done that. Early briefing Monday remember but keep your mobile close. We need to act swiftly when we receive the data or find out where our missing couple is."

Owen left and Cyril checked his watch, dinner date with Julie in exactly two hours. He had time to hand things over and walk home but he had a clear feeling that he would see his desk again early the next day. It was ever thus!

***

The Stray was deserted. The periphery lights left vast swathes in darkness. The driver parked some distance from the Stray Agency building before going to the side door of the van. He slipped on a black, hooded jacket and a pair of oversized shoes. The left one he placed on his right foot and the right on his left; it would bring a moment's confusion for the CSI people, he thought, if they were to turn up. He picked up the air rifle and carefully broke open the barrel before inserting his home made dart. The safety was applied and he was ready. He slipped the gun into a black sleeve.

Keeping out of the light, he moved onto The Stray. The light above the main door was still on and the light in the hall, as always, illuminated the stained glass immediately above the door. All other rooms were in darkness. He removed the air rifle from the sleeve. An occasional car passed on the far edge of The Stray but there was, as hoped, little activity at three in the morning.

Bringing the stock to his shoulder, he looked through the telescopic sight bringing the coloured, glazed window into magnified view. He focussed the sight carefully before bringing the upper, small window to fill it; the eye of God stared back defiantly down the scope. He steadied his breathing knowing that he had only one chance. He lowered the gun. He took one full look around before bringing the sight in line with the target. His thumb flicked the safety off as his finger gently squeezed the trigger. The popping sound seemed louder in the quiet of the night. He then heard the faint sound of breaking glass, which brought an immediate smile to his face, until the siren's wail of a distant emergency vehicle made his heart flutter. He lowered the gun to his side as he crouched low. To his relief, he realised that the wailing sound was heading away from and not towards him. He brought the scope again to his eye and focussed on the target.

The dart had penetrated the lower left piece of lead that surrounded the eye, removing a small piece of glass in the process. There had been only a few stray pieces of glass entering the hall and the alarm remained silent. As quickly as possible he sleeved the gun and returned to the van. Tomorrow the damage would be reported and another game would begin.

***

The warmth emanated from Cyril's naked body as Julie slipped her knees like a piece of a jigsaw puzzle into his, whilst one arm wrapped over his waist. His deep, rhythmic breathing gave her a sense of security. She lay there for a while enjoying his warm scent.

It was still dark when she carefully slipped out of bed. Cyril stirred but did not wake; he simply rolled onto the warm sheets she had vacated. She checked the bedside clock, it was 06:50. She stretched and slipped on a dressing gown before sauntering into the kitchen. Cyril's electronic cigarette was on the worktop, linked by its umbilical cord to the socket. A small, green eye winked as if seeking attention. She picked it up placing it between her lips and pressed the button. The sickly sweet, menthol flavour struck the back of her throat and she started to cough.

"Bad for you that and besides you don't have any vices, Pritchett, that's what you keep telling me. Put it down before it kills you!"

Julie laughed and coughed at the same time, whilst tears ran down her cheeks. "Bloody hell, Cyril, that's disgusting."

"Would you like to bring it here and I'll show you how it should be done without coughing and spluttering over everyone and disturbing the innocent?"

Still coughing she unplugged the device and took it to Cyril who immediately grabbed her hand. "Resuscitation is in order, I think," before pulling her back to the bed. The e-cigarette was forgotten.

A low sun penetrated the small apertures of the Venetian blinds patterning the far wall. Cyril stared at them and exhaled the minty vapour. Julie was tucked under the quilt; the roles were reversed. He slipped out of bed, put on a dressing gown and retrieved his phone from his jacket. To his relief there were no messages. He needed a coffee.

***

Christina Cameron unlocked the front door to the Stray Agency and hit the alarm key buttons, silencing the annoying beep before heading up the stairs to the first landing. Three small pieces of coloured glass lay under the window. She glanced up at the eye of

God to see the piece of bicycle spoke protruding from the lead. A crack ran from one side of the glass to the other and three smaller fractures bled into the edge. She returned to her office. She neither wanted to report the damage nor inform Frederick. She wanted him to find it. He was due in at ten. She'd simply make a coffee and wait for the outcry!

***

The thumping in her head seemed unbearable. Liz could neither move her arms nor her legs. She knew that she was horizontal and that her arms were above her head but she had little free movement. She also realised that she was dressed in a one-piece paper suit. She opened her eyes slowly and the little light there was gave her no clue as to her location. She was scared, hurt and frightened. Her mind focussed on the last moments of consciousness. She remembered the coffee and then the feeling that the room was swirling. She had seen the painting and the silly little figures. It was then that she vaguely recalled Cameron's smiling face as the needle was slowly inserted into her arm. After that everything seemed jumbled and unreal. She pulled at the ties that held her but she had little strength or will. A small bell sounded in some distant place. She suddenly felt anxious, a feeling of nausea flooded her stomach again. As she relaxed the bell stopped ringing.

A silhouetted figure appeared at the doorway. Liz tried to focus on the movement within the darkness but she discerned nothing. She felt the warmth of a hand gently wrap behind her head and lift her. For a moment she was more uncomfortable and she wriggled. She heard the bell again.

"The more you move, the more we hear."

"Drink this, it will help." A straw was placed between her lips.

She filled her mouth trying to taste whatever she had been offered; it was milk. She swallowed and drank again.

"This is only something to help you relax, nothing like before."

Liz tried to focus on the face but the lack of light made it impossible. She uttered feeble thanks and then kicked herself. She drank more and then her head was returned to the pillow. She watched as the figure moved to the door. The true darkness returned.

***

As Christina heard the key enter the lock, she removed her feet from the desk and turned to face the computer screen.

"Morning, Mr Grant."

"That brass sign needs a bloody good polish. I've just noticed. I'd be grateful if you've got a minute this morning, Christina, if you'd give it a bit of a rub."

She had to stop herself thinking, *and what about the brass?* The image didn't sit comfortably. She had already been far too accommodating in securing this job.

"Gives the place a bad impression. Coffee when you've a mo." He headed up the stairs.

"Certainly, Mr Grant." She raised her eyebrows and waited for the exclamation but it didn't come. It appeared that his powers of observation had been exhausted before he had even crossed the building's threshold. He hadn't even popped his head round the office door. She went to the kitchen area and prepared the coffee.

Grant was going through the post when she knocked and brought in his cup. "London trip go as expected?"

"Late bloody trains! What time's the police sergeant due next week?"

"Monday at three. They seemed annoyed that you were unavailable last week." Christina smiled.

"Everything has to revolve round them. I've had that meeting organised for a week, I was damned if I was going to cancel."

"Have you broken something this morning, Mr Grant? There appears to be some glass on the stairs."

Picking up his cup, Grant sipped the coffee. He simply shook his head. She turned to leave. Once on the top step she gave a little, melodramatic squeal.

"Christina, are you alright?"

"Come and look at this!"

Grant moved from behind his desk. He stood behind her and followed Christina's gaze. He then noticed what she was looking at. The upper stained glass was cracked. Where the section had been removed, clear daylight contrasted with the yellow of the surrounding area.

"Jesus Christ what the bloody hell!" He pointed to the thin metal that protruded from the surrounding lead. He walked down the stairs and retrieved a piece of glass. "Fucking vandals!" he yelled. "Do they know what these bloody things cost? Irreplaceable, they're, irreplaceable."

"Do you want me to ring the police?" Christina looked down at him with an expression of total horror. "I love this window and so do most people who come here. Can it be repaired?"

"I don't know. The police? Too bloody right I want the bloody police. Let's see if they're as quick to get here when the bloody boot's on the other foot."

Christina dialled 101 and went through the reporting procedure. She was assured that someone would call within the hour.

***

Cyril had promised Julie that he would accompany her on her shopping trip; he was thrilled. Within minutes of leaving, his phone alerted him to a text.

Dan Rowney's damaged laptop found 300 metres from the car. Forensics have removed the vehicle. Further checks following on both items. No sign of Rowney or Johnson. Following leads from ANPR data, nothing as yet. Further work at site continues.

Cyril just smiled at Julie. "It's from Smirthwaite. Sorry, it's work! Our search goes on and that reminds me, anything from the pins?"

"It's Saturday, it's relax day, shopping day, together day, no cops or corpses, remember. Now, Cyril, repeat after me… no cops." She laughed and linked Cyril's arm.

***

Charles stared down at the van parked in the farmyard. His finely manicured fingers tapped the glass to some irregular rhythm before he wandered down to the kitchen. Three people sat around a small table and their conversation stopped as he entered.

"Dan, Karen, how lovely to see you both again. I take it all went beautifully?" His voice had but the faintest edge to it. He held out his huge fist and shook Dan's hand. "All set for Monday morning?"

Dan nodded. "All set. Police have everything they need."

We have some filming in an hour, you'll need your clapper board and a broad mind. We're filming a montage. Exciting," Charles exaggerated the vowels drawing out the word.

Dan moved back to the table. He now knew what was on the agenda.

Charles reverted to his genteel, camp persona.

"Come Karen, Charlie needs a hug and a kissy."

Karen's demeanour conveyed fear and uncertainty. She had no idea in what Dan was involved. She was an innocent swept along on a fast-running tide, buoyed only by Dan's ever-weakening assurances that all would be well and that he could handle it. If she were honest with herself, she had no idea what he was attempting to handle. From the moment the people had arrived at their apartment her life had become a maelstrom of gut-wrenching uncertainty and absolute fear. Dan had advised her to keep calm and say nothing.

She stood and reluctantly moved round the table. Charles stooped and kissed her on each cheek. As he released her, he turned to the remaining person in the room. His voice changed yet again. "And you? Were you successful?"

"Right through God's eye as requested. The bonus was there was no alarm. Couldn't believe it! The dart lodged in the lead stuff on the edge of all the glass pieces."

"It's called came, lead, came. Daddy is so pleased."

Charles almost skipped from the room, crossed the farmyard and entered what was once a barn. It was partitioned into different rooms, more a studio than a barn. Lighting hung from a scaffolding gantry that was suspended from the skeletal, wooden eaves. The external roof was a mass of solar panels as were the other farm buildings. It fed the heating for the cannabis production.

Two people were already setting up the room. A large table was placed in the centre on which were positioned two Venetian masks. A camera was set to the side and one towards the front. The skill was to keep both cameras out of shot, but if errors were made they would be removed in the editing. There was nothing else apart from a microphone hanging out of shot above the table.

"Have you chosen one of our new arrivals?"

Carla turned to greet Charles. "The one you suggested, the pretty one."

Carla Bonhomme had worked for Charles for a number of years, usually in her hometown of Cannes. Once fascinated by the big screen, she had slowly succumbed to a more base form of cinema. It allowed her to support her drug habit.

"Our other guest, she ready too?"

"She's still out of it and therefore compliant. I suggest we work it like this."

Charles had discovered early in his career that short, pornographic films were a lucrative form of advertising the merchandise he held. They whetted the punters' appetites he would say. The only difference between then and now was the professionalism of the set up and the distribution. They sat and discussed the schedule for the day's filming after which, Charles simply laughed.

"Perfect, my dear. Absolutely perfect." His smile said everything about the man. He stood and kissed her cheeks. "Now, show me the farm. Please your Uncle Charlie."

Chapter Thirteen

Harrogate Police Station was a beacon of artificial light against the autumnal dark as Cyril turned left onto Beckwith Head Road. There was a definite chill in the early morning air and his collar was up. Vapour escaped from his nostrils as he inhaled his e-cigarette. Within five minutes he was checking the boards in the Incident Room. The live link had been established with the tech boys at Newby Wiske and they were ready to view the data as it came live on the large screen. Cyril had asked a number of his team to be present and ready for immediate action; he also had the emergency services ready and a firearms' team should the need arise. He felt nervous, unusually so.

Owen stumbled through the door carrying a cup and saucer and his mug. He looked to all intents and purposes to have been dragged through a hedge backwards.

"Morning everyone." He smiled whilst dribbling whatever his mug held. "Tea, Sir? Cup's clean, washed it myself."

Cyril went to help Owen by holding the door but stood away from the cascading fluid. Shakti followed within minutes. She took a deep breath.

"What are we expecting, Sir?"

Cyril just raised his eyebrows. "That's anyone's guess but we're ready for any eventuality."

"Probably more than can be said for Liz," Owen mumbled into his mug, "especially after the weekend she's had! By the way, has anyone seen her this morning? Anyone heard from her?"

Shakti detected a hint of jealousy in his voice. She knew that they were professionally very close and dared not say that she had called Liz three times that morning with no response other than her answer phone.

Smirthwaite, Nixon and Parks all entered and either nodded, grumbled some inaudible greeting or remained silent. There was definitely an air of anxiety that seemed to intensify as the clock moved on.

Owen took out his phone and dialled Liz's number. It went straight to answerphone. He looked at Shakti and mouthed the word 'Liz'.

Shakti just raised her shoulders and shook her head whilst stretching her mouth downwards; she too felt Owen's anxiety. To make matters worse, he had never known her be late for anything before, if the truth were known she was usually first in, organised and ready.

Why Cyril tapped his electronic cigarette on the table only he knew, probably habit, as there was little noise. The tapping was a welcome distraction for Owen until, however, Cyril spoke and mentioned Liz's name. A multi-directional microphone sat in the centre of the table in readiness for the live link.

"One of our aircraft is missing. Anyone seen Liz?" Cyril enquired.

The collective looked around as if she might be hiding. It clearly showed the tension. Owen could feel the sweat bead on his temples… somehow he had a very uncomfortable feeling that things were just not right.

"We'll start." Cyril glanced at his watch and then at the screen before smiling at DC Smirthwaite, who stood and began the briefing.

"A laptop was found near the vehicle just outside Netherthong, the hard drive had been completely wiped. Some DNA recovered was a match to the DNA found in the car, so we're assuming Dan Rowney. Samples have been taken from his apartment for comparison. Curiously, the laptop delivered to Newby Wiske purporting to be belonging to Valerie Atkins, contained traces of the same DNA, but and more importantly, no match traced links it with Valerie Atkins. According to the lab, she had never touched it. However, the pad does show a match but there's nothing of value stored; the data's been checked and is detailed. It can be found in file 6F of your folder. Look in a minute, please, as there's quite a bit more to get through and time's pressing on."

Cyril took a moment and glanced again at the door, expecting Liz to come bounding in, but it remained closed. Smirthwaite continued.

"Data from NPRC shows four dark-coloured Range Rovers in the area; all accounted for. They are owned by keepers who have never been near the cameras in question; one car hasn't been out of the garage since the owner passed away three months ago!"

"Where are they located?" Owen asked.

Smirthwaite read the list "Scotland, Cornwall, London and Essex. We also cannot rule out from the Forensic reports on the laptop handed to Liz, that the data we are about to see belongs to Valerie Atkins. I checked back through the records and noted that a Miss Dorothy Allen was interviewed at Atkins's crime scene. That interview is filed 12A but I point out that after a further interview, she gave a more detailed description of the man who followed Atkins into the shrubs that night. It's tagged 12B. It's worth noting his hair colour, bleached blond and his size and height. Over six three. She recalled his height against the lamppost as he passed. He was, according to the witness," Smirthwaite looked down and read from the file. "a handsome specimen of a man. May I suggest we reserve judgement until we see this data."

"Thanks, Brian! Everyone catch up on the notes afterwards, please." Cyril checked his watch giving it a brief shake. There were five more minutes before the emergency contact would allow access to the data. He looked at the door. "Still no Liz. That's unusual." The apprehension was growing and he felt the adrenalin rush, it was a key part of why he loved his job.

Cyril's phone vibrated on the table. He raised a finger and then picked up the phone.

"Bennett." He listened before replying, his voice rose. "What? Saturday? So why are we receiving this information that could be crucial to my investigation only now, forty-eight hours after the event? Thanks, get Forensics there and close off the area directly in front of the building. I want an officer with Grant and his secretary until we arrive."

Cyril looked back at the inquisitive eyes that were now locked on him.

"Another piece of tangible evidence found, another bicycle spoke, well, part of one's been fired through the stained glass window of the Stray Agency. Coincidentally, ironically or cynically, it shattered the image of an eye. Only just come through, put on the back burner. Some bright spark thought it was just the work of kids and didn't follow up!" He shook his head. "To think we invest millions in technology to prevent this type of cock-up."

Shakti's demeanour changed as soon as she heard where the incident had occurred and she could not avoid Owen's gaze, which slowly intensified.

"What is…" Owen never finished his query.

"We're live," Cyril interrupted him whilst pointing to the large screen.

The images appeared live. The camera had been focussed onto the computer screen held at Newby Wiske and they watched the password being entered. The screen changed and the arrow magically swept and hovered above the icon of a magnifying glass before a drop box appeared to inform them that the passwords and secure notes were now accessible.

"What do you want first?" the voice requested through the speakers.

Cyril leaned towards the microphone. "Notes please, we'll leave the passwords until later. Let's just see what files come up."

Once clicked on, the only thing that appeared was a small icon with the title that ended with the letters 'MOV'

"Open that, please," Cyril requested.

They heard the double click and the *Quicktime* icon bounced before the black rectangle appeared to the left of the screen.

"Play it!" Cyril demanded.

The arrow moved down to the controls and the triangle control changed to two vertical lines. An image appeared. There was an immediate realisation that they had seen it before. A young, coloured girl was prostrate, stomach down across a large table. Her fingers feebly gripped the far edge and she appeared to be stretched on her toes. The sound of skin slapping on skin was a nauseating accompaniment. The camera angle changed, and they were now looking at the covered girl's face. The Venetian mask, white and glittering, contrasted with her dark, oiled skin. The sound of her discomfort was palpable as she gasped and cried. Slowly the screen dimmed before turning completely black.

As an image returned, the scene was very different. Valerie Atkins was standing in front of three young African girls dressed in their national costume. Bizarrely, each wore a different Venetian mask.

"That's Valerie Atkins. Pause it! Pause it!"

The arrow levitated over the two vertical lines on screen and the image was paused.

"I can now only assume we are looking at a recording. The opening shot is similar to the scenes shown on the four videos found belonging to and including Atkins. Start it, please,"

Valerie began introducing the girls one at a time. Her manner was professional and relaxed as if being in front of a camera was the most natural thing. Each girl introduced herself, stated her age, her ambitions now that she was in the United Kingdom, her hobbies and her skills. Their voices were muffled by the masks. It reminded Cyril of the early beauty pageants. After each girl had been interviewed, Valerie asked if there were one last thing they wished to tell the viewers. Each girl answered with the same statement. *I'm happy, I'm here and I'm a virgin.* It was clearly rehearsed, probably untrue and from the girl's delivery, it was evident that they had little understanding of the statement's significance. Each girl left the stage after her interview but returned to make an appearance at the end. Each was naked apart from the masks. It was at this stage that Valerie turned to the camera and started the selling process but she did not finish as the programme slowly faded.

Within moments an image began to reappear, returning to the girl on the table. Although everything seemed the same, the girl was different. She was fair- skinned, her hands hung almost lifelessly on the table's surface, only moving in rhythm with the bodily pounding. A hand suddenly moved into shot before removing the mask. Liz's face was expressionless, her mouth slightly open and her tongue was just visible, lolling uncontrollably. Her eyes remained closed.

It was surprising how long it took for the people in the Incident Room to realise the identity of the exposed girl's face. It was Owen who screamed first followed quickly by Shakti.

"Stop it now! That's Liz. Somehow they have Liz. Fucking turn the bloody thing off!"

Shakti stood and switched off the screen before turning first to look at Cyril. Guilt, fear and tears were clearly visible in her eyes. Sheturned her gaze to Owen whose bulk was now shaking either through shock or anger or both. She studied his face, looking for the pallor brought on by shock to appear, but his complexion remained deep red. She noticed too that the veins stood out on his neck as he opened and closed his clenched fists.

"What the fuck is going on?" Owen screamed, pointing at the screen.

Nobody answered and nobody spoke. Those who had turned to view the screen were now clearly focussing on Cyril, anxious to hear what he had to say. A slight buzz drifted from other parts of the building, amplified by the vacuum-like state of the Incident Room.

"Listen! Owen!" Cyril's raised voice cloaked a calm instruction that made Owen sit.

Owen turned to look at Cyril, his natural colour returning. "I'm under control, Sir, sorry."

Everyone seemed to either nod or wave away his apology; he was not alone, they all felt his anger. Liz had gained the respect of all the team and everyone was shocked by what they had just witnessed.

An officer dashed in and spoke quietly in Cyril's ear. He nodded.

"Everyone discuss what you have just witnessed, particularly the role played by Atkins. Rerun it over and look for any clues. Go through the files. What we can't afford at this stage is to be distracted from finding the murderer, but now, more importantly, we need to find one of our own who's clearly in harm's way. She needs your policing skills and your professionalism now more than at any other time and we mustn't let her down." Cyril stood. "The Chief Constable needs to speak with me. Everyone please remain, I'll not be long." Cyril was clearly in control as he spoke slowly and quietly. He rested his hand on Owen's shoulder as he spoke. Owen felt Cyril's grip close reassuringly and he knew that if anyone could find Liz, then Cyril would.

Owen responded immediately. "Well what are we waiting for?"

There was a sudden, frenetic burst of voices as if someone had turned up the volume. Cyril turned to leave the room. He paused at the door. "Shakti, chase up Liz's phone records now and see if you can get a trace on the last call that was made from it and also to it."

She immediately left the room to initiate Cyril's request before Cyril followed.

Shakti thought that her number would probably be the last recorded as she had tried to contact Liz several times before the meeting.

Once in his office, Cyril relaxed a little. The images he had just witnessed replayed in his mind and he felt nauseous. For a brief moment, he could let his façade slip and in the privacy of his room, he gave way to his emotions until the expected call came. Cyril listened and made the occasional comment but finished the conversation with a flurry of sentences; they were short and sharp. He explained the news regarding the bicycle spoke discovered in the Stray Agency window. He also made sure that he expressed his anger at the tardy police liaison, strongly pointing out that the information had taken a full forty-eight hours to be processed. He emphasised that the Agency was the last place that Liz had visited on Friday afternoon. It was also obvious that the video had been recorded and sent to the laptop whilst it was in the care of the Digital Forensic Team. He did not want to accept the possible explanation regarding cloud storage that his superior had proffered; to be honest, at this moment, he neither wished to know nor cared, he simply wanted to get on with his mission to find Liz.

The call over, he dialled the National Crime Agency, having been given the instruction to contact a DCI Ged McArdle, the on-call officer working within the Anti Kidnap and Extortion Unit. The conversation was brief, but Cyril was assured that one of the NCA team would be in Harrogate by the following day. Cyril had mixed feelings, but he was prepared to share the stage with the cast from the film *Gandhi* if it would help Liz. What he knew for sure was that Owen was to remain firmly at his side.

On returning to the Incident Room, he was pleased to observe the frenetic activity. He tapped his cigarette on the white board. "What do we have?"

Shakti stood. "Phone records." She pointed to the large computer screen. "Last voice call was to my mobile at 15:21 on Friday afternoon. Liz sounded over the moon that the meeting with Grant couldn't take place. He was late back from London, some kind of rail delay. We're checking now. She said she was going back to the flat. Owen was here with me and heard her. She sounded really excited and upbeat. However, she sent a text to a guy called Jim, with whom she had communicated regularly over the preceding days. The last one was sent on Friday at 15:50." She turned to the screen and Cyril read the text.

'Jim, something serious has cropped up at work and I can't make it this weekend. Sooooo sorry. I'll make it up to you. It'll be worth the

wait, believe me! Don't call me before Monday. You know the work I do. Just think about what's waiting. When you get this show, you love me and understand by sending just a kiss. Pook xxxx.'

"I want Jim found and in here and I want a full analysis of the text message. Sent it to the scribblers at Scientific Support. Ask them to check if the same person sent them all.

She looked enquiringly at Cyril.

"Ever sent a text on a friend's phone and signed it from them?"

She nodded. "We all have our own way of texting… it's worth a look.

"Then you and Nixon contact Forensics and get down to Liz's flat. The usual, no one enters until everything is set. Full report back here as soon as."

Cyril set his team in motion with specific instructions, before contacting the technical officer who had established the live link. He requested a thorough trawl and detailed reports of everything found on the laptop. However, a startling piece of information just confirmed by Forensics, shook him. After scrutiny of the DNA taken from Colin Coulson's personal computer recovered from his apartment, a match had been found on Dan Rowney's laptop and in his car. It took a while for the information to equate.

"You'd be amazed at the shit that's splattered all over computers, dirtier than the average domestic bog. Just think of how many times people sneeze or cough whilst typing. Hairs accumulate within the key gaps. I could go on. Thought you should know now. That's why we were certain that Atkins had never touched the laptop that was allegedly hers."

Cyril hung up, stared at the phone and then the laptop. *That bastard is linked with both murders, as cool as a cucumber, he offers critical evidence that implicates him up to his bloody oxsters*, he thought to himself .

He immediately put out a national alert for Dan Rowney. Within an hour, Rowney's image would be in the hands of the press and the national media. Police had also checked the inventory of the computer equipment held by Rowney's employer, alongside a full search of the premises.

***

Charles sat opposite Dan. Neither spoke, they simply looked at each other. To the observers it was like watching chess without the board or the pieces but it still seemed to be a game of skill if not cunning. Neither wanted to make the first move. Dan smiled and was the first to speak.

"All the info, or should I say, the info you want them to see should be in their hands."

Karen walked in and placed two mugs of coffee on the table.

"What progress on Valerie's computer?" Dan sipped his coffee and smiled at Karen, mouthing the word, *thanks.*

Charles did not move, he just stared at Dan, before answering. The pause was palpable. "Fuck all. If we don't locate it, this place closes within three days. Reverts to tomatoes for Christ's sake, fucking tomatoes. From green to red." He too turned to Karen. "Like bloody traffic signals."

He then took a swig from the mug before leaning across the table. He tapped the surface with his finger, a foot from Dan's hands, as if making a phantom 'check' move.

"You're all over the Internet as we speak. The North Yorkshire Police web page has your mug shot. Pretty, I've got to admit! So, my friend, you leave like our young people enter." He slipped his hand into his shirt pocket and removed a box of Quells. Heard on the vine that you don't like boats."

Dan remained quiet for a moment, sipped more coffee then replied. "And if you find the laptop who's going to get into it?" Dan followed suit, stretched across and tapped the table. "If I'm gone, you…?" His lips broke into an arrogant smile. "Firstly, I'm not getting on any flimsy, blow up, seaside boat and quite frankly, you…" He tapped the table a second time. "Know fuck all about comp…"

For a big man Charles could move quickly and Dan only caught a glimpse of the fist milliseconds before his nose exploded.

He literally saw stars as the intense pain shot from between his eyes, quickly followed by myriad flashing lights that seemed to penetrate his every nerve cell. His chair tipped backwards but his knees caught the underside of the table, springing him back in Charles's direction. Blood spattered a broad area of the table's surface as the force of his moving head flung the warm fluid in a crimson arc. Charles was eagerly waiting to make a second, more devastating strike. This time, he stood and took hold of the back of Dan's head before ramming it onto the ceramic mug rim that was still at arm's length in front of him. It cracked. The sharp edge of the breaking mug was swift in slicing eye and flesh in an almost perfect circle. Dan's face met the table surface with the force generated by Charles's full strength. The crashing remnants of the mug clattered onto the floor, to be swiftly followed by the dull thud of Dan's head making contact with the wood and pottery pieces. Blood and coffee mixed rapidly and the mud-red stream ran and dripped before pooling on the floor. Charles simply uttered the words "Check fucking mate you arsehole."

Karen was frozen to the spot and stared at the havoc caused within the blinking of an eye. It had come from nowhere and was over in no time. She timidly glanced at Charles who was studying one of his nails.

"The bastard has chipped the varnish." His voice, now camp and gentle, sounded as if nothing out of the ordinary had occurred. He slammed his other clenched fist down onto Dan's lifeless left temple. He picked up the box of travel sickness tablets.

"He'll no longer need these." He tossed them at Karen. "But you most certainly will unless, that is, you have the same plans as your man here."

The box hit Karen on the chest and fell onto the floor, a smear of blood marked her shirt. As a sign of affirmation she quickly bent and picked them up.

"Good, then we'll arrange for you to leave tomorrow. You need to pack. He'll be going too but will only go part way. Did he like fish?"

Charles turned his gaze at the offending, chipped nail before he wagged his fingers as if he were royalty dismissing an annoyance. Karen left quickly.

***

Thankfully, the morning had remained dry. A special constable, standing outside the fluttering police cordon, noticed the tell tale blue flashing strobe lights as Owen approached. He signalled for the car to be parked on the edge of The Stray. As Cyril climbed out he noticed the Scene of Crime Manager and waved.

"Nothing much to be honest. No forced entry, just some damage to that upper window. The eye of God I've been informed. The dart has been home cobbled, and the relevant part is it's a piece of bicycle spoke." He walked to the open side door of one of the vans and retrieved it; it was bagged and tagged.

"You can see that the two plastic fittings have been damaged by the lead on contact but we know what they are, they're from a special type of air gun pellet, we see them fairly frequently, used by poachers. I'm aware of the significance of the spoke and we'll see if it matches the one found and those on the wheel."

"Where's Grant and his secretary?"

"They're inside. Best place for them too. She wonders what all the fuss is over, nothing taken, but he's bloody furious about the damage to his window and the length of time it's taken to get real police officers here."

That was clearly in Cyril's mind too but he said nothing.

"All in all, they make a happy couple. Before you go in you might like to look at this. We either have a yeti loose in Harrogate or our shooter has a bizarre sense of humour."

He took Cyril onto The Stray and pointed to a collection of numbered markers. "Footprints, bloody big ones but also the shoes, if you can call them that, obviously oversized cover-ups. Strangely they were worn on the wrong feet. It's either going to be some tit pratting about or, owing to the spoke, quite sinister."

Cyril signed and logged the time of his visit before entering, following the designated path. The SOCOs were just finishing. Cyril paused and waved again at the SCM who wandered over.

"Have you done a thorough check of the whole building?" he asked, waving his e-cigarette. "Every room?"

"No, the hallway and outside. Nothing missing."

"I want the lot doing, every inch of every room, please."

"You'll need clearance. Cost! Cyril, cost! We, as a staff, are pretty thin on the ground. The costs are not just here and now, the majority lies in the analysis of everything found, you know that! More than my job's worth!"

Cyril gently took hold of his coverall and pulled him closer before whispering. "You might not have heard but one of ours is in grave danger. What they've inflicted on her." He emphasised the word 'her'. "Is quite simply bestial. Full and bloody thorough search today, as this was the last place she visited on Friday afternoon. Emphasise to your team that we don't want to miss a thing." Cyril spread a false smile across his face before straightening the ruffled material of the Crime Scene Manager's body suit. "I'll get Tweedledum and Tweedledeeout of your hair and taken to the station."

Owen sidled up to Cyril to help escort Cameron and Grant to a waiting car. "He's gone a funny colour. What did you say to him?"

"Just brotherly advice, Owen. Sometimes, particularly, first thing on a Monday morning, we can all get a little careless, a little laissez-faire. I just emphasised the need for his full professional application to the job in hand. As I see it, we can afford to make no errors. One other thing…" He looked at his partner. "Failing Liz is not on the option list."

Owen simply nodded before tapping the roof of the car, allowing it to move away. He wondered about the word laissez-faire but didn't want to ask at this particular juncture.

***

Shakti and DC Nixon had arrived to find an identical scenario; blue and white tape stretched across the entrance to Liz's apartments, a rather unimaginative block that looked more prefabricated than built. The only saving grace was the view they offered the residents.

"Second floor, I believe," Nixon said as he checked again the number and the sheet.

"See why you're a detective, detective!" She smiled at him. "I've been here a couple of times. Liz invited me when I started, she sort of took me under her wing. It's now we need to get her back and wrap her in ours."

"Good to see the sense of humour is still in evidence... You're right, I must be a detective, detective!"

They both smiled gaining strength from each other. Nixon held up his warrant card to the officer standing outside of the tape and introduced himself and Shakti. The officer lifted it slightly and they both ducked under.

"CSM is by the entrance. This area's been cleared."

"Morning," Shakti said with a slight smile. "Anything?"

"No forced entry but then we expected that. Everything as it should be." He handed her a small iPad. "Images are on there."

Shakti turned the screen to gain some shade, allowing a clearer view of the images. She flicked through them.

"Keys, phone and mail were on the side table in the hall as well as a coat and overnight case. That's not all, there was an envelope in the coat pocket. It contained some kind of master password and instructions. If you move on the images there's a picture."

Shakti looked at Nixon. She knew exactly what it was. "That shouldn't have been with her."

"It doesn't look like the person who entered went anywhere other than the hall. We've just checked all the post boxes and if you flick on you'll see what was discovered in DS Graydon's."

Shakti carefully studied each image as she flicked through, Nixon looked over her shoulder.

"There!" Nixon's finger pointed to the item.

She touched the screen and spread her fingers, enlarging the image.

"Piece of metal. I'm assuming it to be a bicycle spoke or similar, the tag's interesting... K□NI-MAN DAI, K□NI-MAN BεR AM. I Googled it but you try finding the letters on your keypad! Thinking outside the box, I just put an'o' for the second letter and it came up with a reference to an Anansi story from Sierra Leone. The sentence roughly means, '*If you perceive yourself to be clever, and smart, there will be someone waiting to outsmart you.*' It's written in a Krio language, the language of Sierra Leone."

Nixon scratched his head looking at Shakti quizzically. "Makes absolutely no sense, all we now know is that whoever has Liz considers himself to be a smart arse!"

"Finger prints, DNA?"

"It's all been sent as a priority, trust me."

"Are all these images back at..." she didn't finish her sentence.

"By the wonders of modern technology. Makes our life that little bit easier." He smiled. "Shall I sign you out now?" His patience was somewhat strained, she knew the procedures so why waste his time with banal questions. He held his hand out for the pad before checking his watch.

***

As Owen brought the car to a halt in front of the security gate, Cyril inhaled before releasing two streams of mint-smelling vapour through his nostrils. He stared as the gate lifted.

"Before we do anything else I need coffee. Grant and Co. can bloody well wait."

Driving into the car park, Owen sensed that it was going to be a long day.

Owen ensured that Grant and Cameron were both comfortable in the Reception area before grabbing a couple of coffees. It was decided that they would interview them separately. Cyril could see no possible reason for inflicting Grant's arrogant grumblings and rants on his secretary. If Cooper were right, then she had enough to put up with. Owen would interview Christina Cameron. He read through the interview with John Cooper regarding his assumption that Grant had wandering hands. He was determined to discover whether that were the case. He also wanted to find out about the previous incumbent.

Grant was nursing a coffee when Cyril entered the interview room.

"Sorry for the delay, Mr Grant, you'd be amazed how much police time these simple acts of vandalism consume." The not so subtle point flew over his head. "I believe you were due to meet one of my colleagues on Friday afternoon but your train was delayed. Is that correct?"

"Two days it's taken. Two bloody days and then you have the nerve to tell me that I missed an appointment. I can assure you that I had no meeting planned for Friday." He took out his phone and checked the calendar. Here see, 15:00 today with a DS Graydon. Maybe I can save everyone concerned some time and see her when we're done here?"

Cyril was totally noncommittal. "So you have no recollection nor notification of a meeting scheduled for last Friday?"

"Look Inspector or Chief Inspector, we're going round in circles here. My London trip had been planned for a week and I closed my diary at the end of that week until today, Monday. Ask Christina. Christ you can never rely on the railways at the best of times."

Cyril excused himself for a couple of minutes and consulted Owen. "Sorry, Owen, a minute."

Owen offered an apology and joined Cyril. "Check who made the appointment with Liz on the Friday. See if Grant was aware of that appointment then pop along and give me the answer."

***

"Mr Grant. How long has Christina Cameron been in your employ?

Grant was taken aback by the question. "What's that got to do with a bloody piece of steel breaking my window? Christ it's like being with the Key Stone Cops!"

Cyril said nothing.

"Six months, maybe a little longer."

"Before her?"

"I don't really see…"

"Before her? I'll not ask again, Mr Grant. Please just answer the questions. The sooner I have the answers, the sooner we can both leave."

"Paula Baker, left after nine months. Didn't like the work."

"We'll take her details later to confirm all of this."

"She was pregnant. It was mine but she got rid of it. Cost me the price of a small car. I wasn't happy, just one of those things; takes two to tango."

There was a knock and Owen put his head round. "A minute?"

"She made the appointment and believed that she'd added it to his diary on the day before he left for London but she isn't sure. If there was an error it was on her part. She sends her apologies." Owen smiled.

***

"Mr Grant, I believe your secretary made the appointment but might have failed to notify you. DS Graydon visited your offices on Friday at three and was informed that you were delayed. That delay was cited as the reason that the appointment couldn't take place. Now since that appointment, DS Graydon has neither been heard from nor seen and that's why we're conducting a thorough search of your premises. We'll also be searching your home and any other property you may have.

"You can't…"

Cyril held up his finger and Grant subsided. "Furthermore, we'll need fingerprints and a DNA sample just so we can distinguish you from others."

"Bloody hell, man, hundreds of people come through my door. Are you going to take their prints and DNA too?"

"Anyone coming to see you will be in your diary so the answer is simple, yes!"

Grant raised his eyebrows as if asking God for strength. "You must do what you must do. I've nothing to hide."

Cyril noticed the dark sweat marks on his shirt, not only under his arms but also along his chest. "Too warm in here for you, Mr Grant?"

Grant didn't answer. He just folded his arms.

"Once we've done the prints and DNA you may leave."

Chapter Fourteen

Charles watched as Dan's naked body was loaded onto a flat-bed farm trailer next to that of Karen Johnson and covered with a tarpaulin. *Shit happens!* he thought. *Some girls seem to mix with the wrong type of man.* The tractor pulled away, making the trailer start with a jolt. A limp arm fell from under the cover and seemed to wave as the wheels bounced on the cobbles. Her death had not been pleasant; he had allowed the farm lads free reign for the morning before finishing the deed with his own hands there in the studio under the bright lights. Charles loved theatre.

It never ceased to amaze him that he could loathe the thought of sex with a woman but when he had his hands around a female neck, he experienced an erection. Even at the point of her dying, he was pondering the reason. It had happened before. Maybe it was the audience. He had caught a glimpse of Carla by one of the cameras; for a woman who filmed the most bestial of acts she looked so sensitive, maybe it was that. It was of little consequence. On reflection he remembered that he had experienced no sexual buzz during Valerie's ordeal. Maybe it was a hands on phenomenon; the wrapping of the neck, the squeezing, or simply the fact that there was an audience. He dismissed the thought.

Charles had been too engrossed in his own theatre to notice that Carla had filmed the whole performance, from the multiple rapes to the final denouement. It would be her secret and she would tell no one. It would be her security blanket if things turned sour. She had been in this game long enough to appreciate the fickle nature of those in charge.

As the initial idea of transporting the bodies to the coast was a little too risky, they were to be buried in a far corner of one of the fields.

Charles returned to the table, the stain made by Dan's blood was still dark on the light oak. He traced the edge with his finger. How he would have loved to witness Bennett's face when he saw Valerie and then his own officer, exposed, vulnerable and abused, all within the same film. The dead and the living together or would Bennett now believe that Graydon was also with the angels? *It's like playing God,* he thought to himself and he smiled.

***

Mrs Atkins was surprised to receive a call from James, her son, but all the same, she felt a fusion of relief and excitement that carried in her voice. He, however, showed no emotion, he simply requested a contact number for John Cooper.

"John's having a bad time of it, James, he's on medication. We've no idea when the Coroner will release our Val's body and the police appear not to have a clue as to who killed her. You'd think in this day and age with all this technology and the like it'd be easy. Your Dad's not well, knocked him well and truly for six. He's gone back on the bottle, four years on the wagon and now look at him! He's not eating and not shaving. Anyway, how are you?"

"I received a parcel, came two days after Val's death."

"Who's it from? What is it?"

"I just need John's number."

His mother gave him the number and he read it back.

"Let me know if they release the body. Look after dad, he's all you have." He hung up.

She suddenly felt old and alone; all her children were gone and her husband was useless. She sat down and wept. She allowed the phone to fall onto the carpet.

***

Even though it was approaching eleven, John was still in bed when the phone rang. Another batch of tablets and a bottle of wine had ensured a full and deep sleep. At first, the ringing seemed to be part of his dream, but then as he surfaced reality struck and he raised himself onto one elbow before grabbing the phone. He listened.

"John Cooper?"

"Who is it?"

***

The police car dropped Christina Cameron at her flat before taking Grant home. She had shown no objection to her DNA and prints being taken, in fact, she had been more co-operative than Grant. However, she still felt as though she had traversed the deepest of crevasses on the thinnest of ropes. She needed a strong coffee and she needed to contact Charles.

Grant was still confused as to why he was being taken to task for someone disappearing immediately after arriving at an appointment that he knew nothing about. He managed a smile, they had so far been lucky. He wasn't so naïve though as to realise that the sharks were getting a little too close to the boat. Without Valerie Atkins's laptop, an opportunity well and truly lost, it was clearly time to draw in. If they had managed just one more week, then the project would have been finished, out of their hands and ready for the public domain. The revelations would have been explosive and with the shock would come fame, not only for Valerie Atkins, but also for the Stray Agency and with that, for Grant himself. This time, there would have been no conflicting responses from the viewing public. She would only have received praise for blowing the whistle and for exposing the trafficking of people, drugs, prostitution and pornography taking place under everyone's noses.

Grant reached for the phone, at least he'd had the foresight to remove it from his drawer before being asked to leave his office. He dialled the one number that was stored on the SIM. It was dead.

***

Cyril and Owen sat facing each other in the dedicated Incident Room, comparing notes on Grant and Cameron. They were in agreement that she would not remain in Grant's employment after the treatment that she had received. They had both heard Grant grumbling as he left.

Shakti entered with Nixon.

"Sir, you're the very man!"She sat next to Owen. "Grab a couple of coffees Nix and I'll go through our findings. SOCO team has confirmed no break in, no damage. Everything seems to be in order. Her coat and weekend bag were in the hall, keys and mobile on the hall table and she'd even collected the day's mail. It was unopened. The photographs should be through."

She stood and logged onto one of the computers, her fingers danced across the keyboard. She waited, tapping the table with impatience. "Come on for Christ sake!" She then started typing again before waving them over.

"All looks neat and orderly," Nixon added as he placed Shakti's coffee next to the Mickey Mouse, mouse mat.

Cyril slipped on his glasses.

"Bit like the Marie Celeste, no disturbance. Why would the keys be there? Had she locked herself out?" Owen said as confused as the others.

"Perfect really, you kidnap someone, confiscate their belongings which you then deposit back in their home and leave it as if everything's dandy. You check their phone for appointments or unanswered texts or calls. You even send a text message, or get them to send a text to cancel any appointments they might have for the next few days, so giving yourself time before the person is reported missing. It's really that simple. The difficulty is in not being seen or setting off an alarm. They will, however, have left traces on things they've touched, DNA transference. The only thing is it takes time to locate and assess and the one thing we don't have is time! The last place she was seen was the Agency and the last person we know who saw her was Christina Cameron." Cyril stood before Shakti interrupted.

"But she spoke with me after she left the Agency. Owen was with me. She was excited, there was nothing wrong, said she was going home. Unless someone was waiting for her?"

"There would've been blood and snot all over the show had someone tried to do a snatch. Christ, Shakti, she might be bloody small but she's as mean as a honey badger when she's cornered! No, I can't see that." Owen knew her too well.

Shakti skipped onto the next image. "Then there's this, found in her post box." Shakti enlarged it.

Cyril immediately felt a shiver run down his back. As his mother used to say,*as if someone was walking on my grave.*

"The CSM looked up the meaning. Nixon jotted it down. He reported that the note was attached to part of a bicycle spoke."

"And I'll bet you a fiver, Harry Nixon, that it's part of the one that was fired through the eye of God," Owen added.

Nodding, Nixon opened his note pad. "He said it was an Anansi story from Sierra Leone. That sentence means roughly, '*If you perceive yourself to be clever, and smart, there will be someone waiting to outsmart you.*' It's written in a Krio language, the language of Sierra Leone."

Cyril neither appreciated the quote nor the link with Sierra Leone. Without speaking he left the room.

"Was it something I said?" Nixon enquired with genuine concern.

The three turned to watch Cyril go and then exchanged glances, each pulling a face suggesting confusion.

"Had a thought yesterday when the live feed was showing. It might have nothing to do with anything, but was there any record of porn sites on Coulson's computer?" Owen voiced.

"Not that I remember, Stuart Park sorted that. I'll check."

Cyril sat in his office and cupped his face. In his mind's eye he could see a shower of rough diamonds spread across a small table, myriad colours looking more like chunks of broken glass than valuable gems. He reached for the phone. The Chief Constable's Secretary answered.

"Just give me a minute, Cyril, he's searching through a pile of paper for a smaller pile, but first has to shift a half hundredweight of ballast." She giggled. "I'll put you on hold, back in a tick."

Handel's Water Music played, more twang than flow; the thought of running water made Cyril want to pee.

"He's found it, the secret of life. Thankfully the world will continue on its usual orbit and life will remain as we know it, Cyril, but that's our little secret! I'll put you through." Her voice was droll and flat.

"What can I do for you, Cyril?"

Cyril began to explain. One thing was sure, he was never happy with coincidences.

Smirthwaite popped his head round the door. "Grant's story corroborates. His train arrived in Harrogate 15:40, it was delayed. Station CCTV shows him leaving the building and grabbing a cab. Taxi firm has confirmed that he was dropped at home at 16:12. Even gave a generous tip!"

***

John Cooper replaced the phone into the cradle. If the persistent ringing had not brought him to life, then the revelation certainly had. He withdrew a mobile from the bedside cabinet before crossing the room. He extracted a small card wallet from his jeans and from that a SIM card. He popped the card into the phone, switched it on and waited. He could feel his heart beating in his chest. For the first time since Val's death, he felt alert. He noticed that the phone was lit and ready. He dialled.

"Grant it's Cooper. I know where Val's computer is."

There was silence for a moment. Cooper could almost hear the relief on the other end of the phone. "Do I guess or are you goin…"

"She'd posted it to James, her brother. He received it a couple of days after she died. She obviously knew that they were aware that she'd been collecting evidence. As she often said when she came home a total mess, that when you play with fire there will come a time when…."

Grant interrupted. "Your fingers get burnt?"

"No, nothing that simple, she always said, *If you play with fire there'll come a time when he'll roast you in the flames of hell.*"

"Please God tell me it was protected with a password?"

"She'd sent that also, a separate letter arrived a day after the computer. James has seen most of what it contains, he knows everything apart from data stored on a partitioned section of the hard drive; that has a separate, unknown password. He's considering taking it to the local police, sending it anonymously. He doesn't want to get involved. He went on and on about how I'd corrupted her like I'd done to my career and his by all my cheating and lies. Sadly he was right. He knew me too well!"

"Give me his number, now."

***

"You must follow your instincts, Cyril, that's what good police work is, a cocktail of scientific fact, experience and gut feeling. You know that you always have my full support. Is there anything else?"

The conversation neither made Cyril feel more confident nor more sure of his suspicions. He thought back to the doctor. He reflected on the fact that the doctor had disappeared and that his body had never been found. It gnawed at him. He also knew that the man was but a puppet for others and then it struck him. He recalled the name, even though he had never seen nor met the man, but he knew his name, Charles. He closed his eyes before standing and dashing towards the Incident Room.

"I know the murderer's name!" he announced with neither pleasure nor pride. "I've no idea what he looks like, but I know something of his character." He picked up a pen and added the name in block capitals to one of the white boards. "A few years ago we disrupted a major people-smuggling ring, a ring that had its roots in France during the Second World War. The discovery was a coincidence as we were investigating a doctor from Richmond. This brought to light a close- knit people-smuggling ring that had, and this is why I had to leave earlier, its evil tentacles in Sierra Leone."

Cyril explained, emphasising the fact that their enquiries had caused a major impact. They had made some ripples, how large and how far those ripples had affected the group they would never know. He outlined the case. Only one arrest had been made and he must have been released probably last year or earlier this. Some were never traced.

"One was the doctor, from Richmond. No body was ever found, only DNA traces. His housekeeper did very well out of his death, very well indeed. We believe that the operation continued but obviously not on the same scale.

"So the recently freed guy isn't your mysterious Charles, I take it?" Harry Nixon asked.

"No, as I said, it goes back to a previous complex case, one of those where you open one door and three more present themselves. The person in question was a Phillip Jarvis, a student at Ripon Teacher Training College in the seventies. Two bodies of very young babies were discovered buried in the college grounds many years later, during some building works, bringing Jarvis into the spotlight. He was by then working in France. One thing led to another and Jarvis was implicated. He'd developed a profitable sex trade in Ripon, using students during his time there. Two had become pregnant and had refused to have the recommended termination. After a while they decided that they couldn't carry on so they tried to commit suicide by gassing themselves and their babies in a car belonging to the college doctor. Turns out he was having a relationship with Jarvis too. Are you all still with me because you couldn't make this stuff up."

All eyes were still on Cyril.

"Anyway, we discover that the good doctor and Phillip continued to develop their relationship away from Ripon. They became involved in a profitable people trafficking business, at the heart of which, I believe was Charles, the controller. As I said, the doctor disappeared and only his DNA and some body parts were discovered. There was little evidence to implicate Jarvis and the Forensic evidence on the suicide car worked in his favour. Consequently, he received ten years that was reduced. So we've never knowingly seen Charles."

"Do we have a description?" Shakti asked.

"No, as I say, we never heard nor saw him but we knew he was there in control, the Godfather. A pushbike accident in Nice killed the one person we hoped might be able to help; I think it was from her that we got his name. All we know was that Charles had a reputation for being a sadistic bastard."

It was then that a number of pennies dropped into place, bringing an unnerving silence. It was as if no one dared speak first, to burst the bubble of realisation. Finally, Owen spoke.

"Tangible evidence. Pushbike you said, Sir? Tangible evidence or coincidence?"

Cyril tapped his forehead with the palm of his hand. "Yes and hatpins! I've been a fool! Killed using Charles Horner pins!"

"So too have I! Liz's handbag, her handbag wasn't there." Shakti moved to the images of Liz's hall. See, it's missing."

***

James Atkins's phone vibrated in his jacket pocket for the second time in a matter of ten minutes; it was ignored. The class of pupils was his main concern, particularly a small group of girls who consistently tried to derail the lesson to another agenda. He had allowed it at the start of the term, believing foolishly that they were curious and overly enthusiastic to communicate, after all, it was an English lesson. When the interruptions started to take over his planning he decided it should stop. It was then that he faced a more organised form of Year Eight anarchy. In some ways it amused him, but in truth it was affecting his coverage of the curriculum. He was just about to ask one of the girls to leave the room, divide and rule being his new mantra, when the phone vibrated yet again.

He turned away from the class and removed his phone. He didn't recognise the number but whoever it might be had left three messages. It would have to wait.

The bell echoed outside in the corridor and Pavlov's alarm, as he called it, immediately brought a more understandable disturbance within the class of clattering chairs and raised voices, which, in turn, brought James a degree of relief. He had to admit that this particular class was a real test of his teaching and pupil management skills. As the last child stumbled out of the room, he perched on the edge of the desk and dug for his phone.

He pressed the answer phone, waited then followed the mechanical voice's instructions.

"Mr Atkins, we've never met and I'm sorry for the intrusion. My name is Grant, Frederick Grant. Please give my number a call, it's of the utmost urgency that we communicate as soon as possible."

He listened to the other messages and they were all very similar. He checked his watch, he had an hour for lunch and so he dialled.

"May I speak to a Frederick Grant."

"Mr Atkins thanks so much for getting back to me." Knowing the quality of James' relationship with his sister, he decided not to offer condolences. "I'll not waste your time. I'm your sister's agent or should I say I was, before her sad and untimely death…"

"Murder, Mr Grant, murder."

"Yes, yes, her dreadful murder. She was working on an extremely sensitive documentary about a criminal gang working in and around the Harrogate area. She had, somehow, and to be honest we don't know how, infiltrated this gang." He lied in the hope that it might help his cause. "And from that very dangerous involvement, she amassed a catalogue of incriminating facts. She formulated a draft documentary that was put to selective media clients and as a consequence of the importance and the sensitive nature of the material, one of those clients offered an immediate, unequivocal, commission. It was at that point that we believe that her cover was blown. Her credibility within the group was lost resulting in her murder. I also believe that you have seen and read the evidence she has stored on her computer?"

"I have and to be honest, although I can see the extent of the criminality, it's extremely jumbled and to me makes little sense."

"Believe me, Mr Atkins, it's all there, jig-saw like, I know, but all there. Now we're faced with a dilemma. Sorry, I'll rephrase that, you're faced with a dilemma. You can hand the laptop to me and we can fulfil Valerie's dream and get the programme out there. Obviously, we'll have to have a different presenter but the credits and royalties will be partly hers, I personally believe that's what she would have wished for. The other two concerns are that you might send it to the police and they might, and I emphasise, might, apprehend those responsible for her murder. It wouldn't surprise me, however, if the culprits have already taken the necessary steps to close down their operation and fled. Lastly, a concern that you should give most thought to. They might be like me and have already tracked your location. Should that be the case… well we'll not consider that possibility until you make up your mind as to which path you wish to take. I can relieve you of the baggage today. I can meet you at a place of your choosing by this afternoon. It will then be all over for you."

Atkins considered the ambiguity of his language in the final sentence. "I'll text a time and venue within the next half an hour. The laptop will be placed in a secure location and I'll then text you the details. It'll be up to you when you then collect it. I suggest, if you're not already, that you should be in the Wigan area by mid afternoon. I trust this will be the last I'll hear from you."

"You have my word. Mr Atkins, thank you. I believe your decision today might result in a good deal of police action and a number of the criminal fraternity getting what is only just and fair." He hung up. For the first time in days he felt a sense of relief.

James Atkins felt exactly the opposite; suddenly he felt as though his family had again come to burden him. He went through to his locker and retrieved Valerie's laptop before heading to the IT stockroom to collect a sleeve of discs. As a guarantee he would copy what he could, after which, they were welcome to the bloody thing.

He left the machine running through his first lesson of the afternoon, occasionally changing the disc when necessary. The bell sounded to signal the end of the lesson, he would be free for the rest of the afternoon.

***

Grant was now passing over the M62, the high, Pennine Way footbridge well behind and Winter Hill clearly visible in the distance to his right. He had decided to continue round the M60 and then head north up the M6.

***

James Atkins wrapped the laptop in brown paper and taped it thoroughly adding a label, *For collection by Frederick Grant.* He then began to text.

Parcel ready for collection from St Thomas's Academy. He added the address followed by the instruction. Go to the main Reception, Bill Lyons, caretaker will have the parcel. You will need identification. You must be at the address no earlier than 17:30 and no later that 19:00.

By choosing this as the collection point, James knew that the handover would be recorded on the school CCTV. He had his doubts as to whether Grant's motives were as charitable as he had stated.

***

CCTV footage of the area around the Stray Agency and Liz's apartment had failed to provide any clues. Stuart Park had reported that even though the hard drive had been removed to investigate further Coulson's computer, a deep screening investigation had discovered a hidden logic bomb or slag code. This cleverly concealed a second code that was activated on attempting to clear the first, resulting in the released virus closing down and corrupting all of the stored data. It was now unlikely that they would be able to recover any thing further. The only thing that could be significant was that certain files had been deleted around the time of Coulson's abduction.

"That, more than likely is Dan's handiwork," Stuart Park informed the collective. "Should we discover Atkins's laptop there's also a likelihood that the same viruses will be present." He raised his hands as if to suggest someone had made an error. "At least we've been forewarned and know the nature of the foe."

Most of the computer information passed Cyril by. He just mumbled something about the work of the devil before thanking Stuart. Another day loomed. What they needed now was for the Forensic results to shed light into the dark corners of the criminal world. He also had to plan carefully the next move. Owen checked his watch and flicked on the television. Within minutes, the news broadcast the public appeal made by Cyril earlier in the day. He always found looking at himself on TV to be disconcerting but he watched with care, keen to see if the urgency in his message was conveyed. His request for anyone who had seen anything at either address, no matter how insignificant it might seem, to come forward was clear, but it had been Owen who had suggested that he stress the need for anyone using a dash cam or bicycle helmet cam in the area from Friday 13:00 in the afternoon to noon Saturday to come forward with the memory cards. Liz's on screen photograph with all the contact details the public needed, brought home the solemnity of the moment. Shakti couldn't control herself anymore and burst into tears. It had been a dreadful roller coaster of a day and incredibly stressful.

***

It was dark when Cyril eventually crossed The Stray. He had declined a drink with Owen, it seemed neither appropriate nor desirable. He had work to do, work that just could not wait. His mind was an amalgam of mixed images of a past case blending uncomfortably with the graphic images of Liz.

The intermittent sheets of drizzle spread in waves of varying opacity. He showed little concern as he ducked under the umbrella; his mind was elsewhere. He had found it difficult to talk to Julie about his sudden feelings of professional impotence. He was a copper for Christ's sake, a detective at that and a bloody good one. Were he and the others so personally involved that it was blunting the edge of his normally sharp mind? Should he step back and let others take over?

He nipped through the narrow ginnel linking West Park with Robert Street. He was glad to be home. He put down his laptop, removed his shoes, wiped them and added shoetrees. For once in his career he was looking forward to the arrival of the officer from the NCA in the morning. It would bring a specialist's expertise, a professional detachment that would help focus the investigation. Experience of working within the Anti Kidnap and Extortion Unit could only be a blessing.

***

Grant was later than he thought, even the car's Sat Nav. had decided to take him on a very circuitous journey. He parked in the Visitors' car park; there were no other cars. The lights of the Reception area were bright, reflecting off the wet pathway that led from the car park. He tried the door but it was locked. He then noticed the, *After hours, ring for attention,* sign. Within minutes a young man arrived carrying a brush, followed by a German shepherd dog. He opened the door.

"Can I help?"

"Mr Lyons, Bill? My name is Frederick Grant, I've come to collect..."

"Expecting you." He saw Grant looking warily at the dog. "He's fine; it's his twin you need to worry about but I only bring him when I'm checking the site at night. This one's as daft as a brush, soft as dry sand. Come in and wait there and I'll get the package. The dog 'll stay with you."

Grant stared at the dog. Its upper lip lifted revealing a row of white teeth followed by a shallow growl. Grant took a step backwards before seeing the caretaker returning with the parcel.

"I've been told to check some ID and get you to sign this." He handed over the receipt but kept hold of the parcel. Grant signed, showed his driver licence and took the parcel. The caretaker watched as the look of excitement flushed across the visitor's face.

"That's all there is, Mr Grant."

"Yes, yes, thanks."

Bill showed Grant out, locking the door behind him. The dog stayed at the glazed door, its breath misting the window until Grant had driven away. James Atkins came out of the room behind the Reception desk as the lights from Grant's car moved away towards the school gates. Bill Lyons reappeared.

"Was that him, James?' Bill quizzed as he called the dog. "Seemed a bit eager and overly excited. What you give him, a hundred grand?" Both men laughed.

"Easy to make a desperate man happy, just give him what he thought he'd lost." He smiled. "Thanks, Bill. I'll be fifteen minutes and I'll be gone, I'll give you a shout."

"It was nothing, just remember me at Christmas!" Bill said, chuckling to himself before calling the dog. "By the way, your receipt!"

James returned to the office and photocopied it. The CCTV camera recorded in five minute blocks, enabling easy tracking of the images. James scanned through the files and identified the section of tape featuring Grant. He copied the relevant footage onto a memory stick.

***

Grant turned onto the A580 and quickly glanced at the parcel lying securely on the passenger seat. At last he had the laptop. He felt a sudden burst of elation. He looked up as if to give thanks for the manna that had finally landed into his hands. In three hours he would be home.

***

Reading through the case notes, Cyril was surprised as to how quickly the time had flown by. Had he really known Owen and Liz that long? He also felt a stab of guilt as he considered the evidence balanced against the coincidences within this case and the past one. He was now, more than ever, convinced that his actions so long ago had sown this particular wind. He awaited the tornado.

Chapter Fifteen

Liz sat on the mattress, her knees under her chin. One arm enwrapped them as if she were offering herself a degree of security; the other was shackled to a metal ring set on the wall. She was sore and had been bleeding but that thankfully had stopped. However, she was reluctant to pee, the burn was excruciating. She assumed that she had been raped, but she had no recollection of the incident nor of anything that had happened to her. Her impressions seemed vague and unreliable. She had tried to recollect, but it had only been over the last few hours that she had been able to visualise her past through piecemeal recollections that seemed neither clear nor credible. She could see Owen, but she was unsure of exactly who he was. She remembered his saying something about a French letter. She remembered slapping him and laughing. What were she and this Owen doing with a condom? Strangely and confusingly, she had no difficulties in connecting the term French letter and condom! Her mind played back the moment and as the cocktail of drugs slowly dissipated, she could recall more but for Liz the process was happening far too slowly.

By day at least, Liz had the birds for company. She could often hear them scrabbling in the eaves of the building or calling outside, frenetic, free and alive. It was her only contact with the world she so cherished. It amazed her how things that had seemed so important last week had no intrinsic significance now. What she had taken for granted, when denied, suddenly seemed so very precious. It was now down to a more animalistic form of survival where only the basic bodily functions mattered; the next drink, the next meal, when the stinking bucket would be emptied. The one luxury she treasured was having the security of a thin veil of yellow light glowing throughout the long, cold, night hours. The idea of a change of clothes, washing, breathing fresh air, walking freely in the open air were now gone.

The square window, set high within the rustic brick, allowed some daylight and the evening brought the red glow of the setting sun on the opposite wall, but it afforded little warmth. The wired, opaque glass was too high, too dirty for her to find clues as to her whereabouts. There were some noises; the occasional vehicle, the over-flight of a low aircraft and the quiet chatter of human voices, many foreign, which she could hear just outside the window. This was now her world.

She looked at the three scratch lines that she had added to the wall. They enabled her to keep track of her time alone. She had no awareness as to why she had started marking them, it had been instinctual. She stood, stretched and walked as far as her heavy, wrist-wrapped chain allowed; it was not far. Her world was encapsulated in a triangle comprising the bed, the bucket and the bowl.

She assumed that the building had, at some stage in its past, been a stable block, and her cell was one of the stalls. The walls stopped well short of the roof but they were still high, allowing some distant light to flood into the corners during darkness. On occasion, she could see shadows move across the wooden rafters and exposed red roof tiles, as people moved within the unseen spaces elsewhere in the building. She knew that if it were not for the spilling security of the twenty-four hour light, she would be in a much worse emotional state. She had become, even in such a short time, thankful for small mercies.

She moved herself, sitting more upright as the bolt on the upper part of the door was slid back and opened. A female stared at her, always the same one, always the same emotionless expression. Liz believed them to be about the same age. She smiled in the hope of receiving some kind of human interaction within this twice-daily ritual, but her hopes were dashed. The door closed without a reciprocal smile or a word spoken.

She was determined to remain as positive as possible. She pulled the blanket up over her knees. The now greying, paper coverall offered little protection from the dropping evening temperature. She knew that within half an hour the door would open fully, some food would be added to the bowl, some water placed nearby and the bucket swapped. She closed her eyes trying to recall any specific event, to concentrate on the slap she somehow remembered giving Owen. It was a desperate attempt to see if she could unlock any more of her memory. *Why a French letter?* she asked herself as the bolt was drawn back on the door.

***

The sound of Big Ben's chimes erupted from Cyril's mobile. It was 04:30. The noise didn't wake him, he had beaten his alarm by a good forty minutes. He had showered, shaved, dressed and was on his second coffee. He could not sleep, he just wanted to be in his office and in the Incident Room. He needed to review any new intelligence that had arrived overnight, but most importantly he needed to focus, focus on the most important thing and that was finding Liz. He knew that by finding her he would be a step closer to Charles.

As Cyril crossed The Stray he took a moment to look up; the sky was full of stars, it was clear and cold; so far the walk could be described as bracing, it was the first time this year that he had seen the grass veiled in a fine filigree of ice. It glistened in the yellow streetlights, complementing the star-studded darkness. He filled his lungs with the fresh night air whilst contemplating Liz. *Would she be able to see the stars, to breathe in the air or was she no longer of this earth?* He did not let the thought dwell but set off again at a brisk place, quickly replacing the fresh morning air with the mint flavoured vapour and a dose of nicotine.

People were busy on his arrival; the work of the Harrogate police didn't stop. DC Paul Mortimer did a double take on seeing Cyril enter the Incident Room. He glanced at the clock. "Couldn't sleep, Sir?"

Cyril simply shook his head. "Anything?" Cyril's voice sounded almost pleading.

"Great response from your request for dash cam footage, loads. Going through it now and reg. numbers are being cross-referenced. There are one or two interesting leads that are being chased up. Forensics has come up with some positive DNA matches from Liz's coat. According to those at Hogwart's…"

Cyril pulled a quizzical face, it was too early for games.

"Sorry Sir, my name for The Jeffrey's Building, Forensics, you know. Hogwart's is the school of witchcraft and wizardry."

On a normal day, Cyril would have shown a degree of displeasure but at this time in a morning he was a tad more tolerant. "Go on!"

"The evidence clearly points to the fact that Liz's coat carries a good deal of Christina Cameron's DNA. They assure us that, at some stage, she must have worn it. There's also food detritus, I think we know them as crumbs, detected on one of the leather settees from the Stray Agency and from Liz's coat. More to the point they match! Fabric particles from her coat were found on the settee too."

"Really? Slow down just a little."

"Sorry, always find this stuff exciting, get carried away. You should hear my missus!" Cyril's expression brought an abrupt halt to his domestic musings.

"Drug traces located on the floor in the same room and in the kitchen."

"Do the 'wizards' know which?" Cyril humoured him.

"The Toxicology wizards are the best, Sir. One moment. "He walked over to a computer.

Why he had joined in with the wizardry analogy he would never know but Cyril felt it lift his spirits a little.

"Here we are, take your pick."

Cyril read the list. He pointed to the drug, Ketamin.

"Just a second, says here that traces were found on the floor, and on minute fragments of what are believed to be from a ceramic cup. Incidentally, it was also recorded that there were six saucers but only five cups in the kitchen. No broken cup in the bin either. If they'd damaged a cup recently, it was removed from the place." He scrolled down the report. "Liz's finger prints found on the frame of a painting in the same room, also on door handles and the settee. From the spread, it can be safely assumed that she was there for some time. As a matter of fact, your prints were also found but only in the hall and Grant's office. You might also like to know that we have some prints belonging to John Cooper."

Cyril wasn't too fazed by that information. "We know he's been there, he told me he visited on a number of occasions, so nothing strange in that. What else?"

"It's just that one of his prints overlaps one of yours, suggesting he'd been there last week after your visit."

Cyril raised an eyebrow and sat on the edge of the table. "I want all this stuff ready for the morning briefing, I also want you there. Contact ANPR Control and see what's been processed regarding the cars spotted on the dash cams. The sooner we have that information the better."

Providing that she had arrived on time, Cyril estimated that Liz had left the Agency building at about three thirty, because there had been no appointment. She had phoned Shakti and told her that she was on her way home. Cameron was aware that Grant would not be at the meeting on Friday, so why had she not telephoned Liz and cancelled? If she had forgotten to do that, why would Liz have gone into the other room and possibly have had a drink when everyone knew she was desperate for an early finish and to get home?

"I want Christina Cameron in and I want her in before the sun's up. I want her flat scouring. Please arrange the search and let me know the time it'll happen. And to be safe, I want an armed unit present. I'll clear it now. Get Owen out of bed. I want him there and in charge."

Cyril thought about getting Cooper and Grant in for questioning, but then had second thoughts. He believed that the best course of action would be to get Ruth to bring Cooper in about some fictitious need to identify some of Valerie's belongings. Grant could wait.

***

Christina Cameron's apartment was some distance from the centre of Harrogate. Two cars and an unmarked Police Armed Response Vehicle pulled up outside the Victorian terraced house on King's Road. Owen had already arrived, ready and prepared, he was wearing a ballistic vest that was clearly marked 'Police'. The apartment was on the lower floor. The standard procedure had been well rehearsed, the rear of the building was covered. When everyone was in place, Owen checked the names of the occupants of both apartment she had been handed before he went up and rang the bell. It seemed strange that armed police were close by and yet it was accepted practice to believe the occupier, at this stage at least, was innocent.

His senses were alive as adrenalin coursed through his veins. He rang again keeping his finger on the bell, unsure as to what to expect. An upstairs light came on quickly followed by hands parting the vertical blinds. Anannoyed but reluctant face peered onto the road, suddenly becoming more aware of the blue, flashing strobe lights on the police vehicles lighting the garden and the surrounding buildings intermittently, He looked down onto the path at the three dark figures standing apart, the reflective 'Police' label proudly visible. Owen waved and pointed to the door. Moments later the hallway light illuminated the door's transom window, shedding more light onto the pathway.

The door opened until the security chain snapped at full stretch. A man in his sixties stared out at Owen and then he turned his attention to the figure, positioned a little further down the path dressed in helmet and goggles and holding a gun.

Owen spoke. "Mr Turnbull? Police, open up!"

Confused, the man momentarily retreated before sliding the chain on the back of the door, opening it fully. He immediately put his hands in the air.

Owen could not help but smile, whether it be this reaction or a sense of relief that they were in the building, he was unsure. "Which is the door to Christina Cameron's flat?"

Turnbull lowered one arm before pointing to a door set away from the porch, about halfway down the corridor.

"She's not in, saw her do a flit about eight last night, two bags, said nothing, not even a goodbye. Snooty cow, never liked her. What's she done?"

Owen ushered Turnbull outside before nodding to the officer behind him. Someone brought up an *Enforcer*, a steel ram that made short work of the door lock. The sound of splintering wood could be heard above Turnbull's complaints. He was put into one of the cars for safe-keeping, as a pair of boxer shorts and bare feet were inadequate cover for someone of his age to be standing about in outside on such a chill morning.

Once the apartment was deemed safe, the waiting SOCOs moved in and Mr Turnbull was ushered back upstairs. There would be little chance of sleep; the front door remained open as a constant stream of white-coated figures passed in and out. He watched with curiosity from an upstairs window. Owen appointed an officer to quiz Turnbull about Cameron.

Owen called Harrogate Police Control to initiate a border check and a watch on all single females matching Cameron's description. He was under no illusions. By now, if her name was not Cameron, she would have reverted to her original name or be travelling under a false passport. She could be anywhere. After contacting local taxi firms, Owen received a positive identification. Amir Patel had collected a lady from the King's Road address at 19:50 and driven her to Manchester Airport, dropping her at Terminal One. His records showed that he had arrived at 21:47. All she had told the driver was that she was looking forward to visiting relatives; no destination had been mentioned.

That narrowed the border checks considerably and the best match was found, a single female answering to Cameron's general description, travelling first class on Turkish Airlines, departing 23:45 to Ataturk Airport, Istanbul, under the name of Rosalyn Bruce. The ticket had been purchased in the afternoon of the departure day.

***

Cyril peered at the screen on his desk, DC Mortimer had been most efficient. He was watching a dash cam recording taken on Friday evening. It showed a Ford Transit parked close to the Stray Agency. As the vehicle passed the van, the headlights picked up a clear image of a man, carrying what looked like a rolled up carpet. It was only brief but remarkably clear.

Cyril shook his head. *Clichéd crime! Getting rid of a body by wrapping it in a carpet,* he mumbled to himself. *But very effective.* He looked again and paused the film. Unfortunately, the bundle was draped over his left shoulder, the shoulder closer to the road, consequently blocking a clear view of the man's face. He wound back the video until the front of the van was visible and checked the number plate. It was clear and would therefore be tracked within the region's' ANPR data. There was a knock on the door and Cyril didn't turn, expecting it to be Owen. "Stop blocking the light and come and see this wizardry, right up your street! The clarity of these cameras is quite…"

He heard a polite cough. He was wrong, it was not Owen. He turned to see a woman in her early thirties. He then noted the police security neck lanyard.

"DCI Bennett?"

Cyril stood. "Correct and you are?"

"DI Margaret Podmore, National Crime Agency." She checked her watch. "Couldn't sleep and assumed you'd be in the same boat, always happens to those close to the victim. I can come back if you're busy or have an appointment with Owen, was it?"

Cyril held out his hand. "Cyril, Cyril Bennett. Blame my mother for the Cyril bit." He smiled and pulled out a seat.

"And your father for the Bennett? Margaret, but people call me Peg, please feel free. It seems our parents pleased themselves!" She smiled and raised an eyebrow. "I've gone through the files. The crucial thing that I have to ask immediately." She paused. "Have you kept the computer believed to belong to Valerie Atkins open? By that I mean able to receive the Internet? If the person holding Liz is going to communicate, the likelihood is it will be through that."

Cyril immediately picked up the phone and called Newby Wiske, requesting that the technicians responsible for the Atkins's case call him as soon as possible.

Peg continued. "There may be something already waiting in the ether. My experience tells me there is unlikely to be a ransom demand from the evidence I've read. This kidnap hasn't been done for financial reward, and if what you believe is true, it's been done to make a point. Simply put, it's a vendetta. How safe your colleague is at this moment depends on what happened to those working for this Charles fellow. I don't need to spell out the worse case scenario to you. Had they wanted to just kill her, you'd have located Liz's body by now. You have two bodies already so killing is not a problem for them; two or three makes no difference to a man who is used to that depth of criminality, he has nothing further to lose. In my experience, she, Liz, is still alive and held locally, probably within a thirty-mile radius of the point from which she was abducted. Once we know there have been no further communications, we can start formulating a strategy from the evidence we now have and draw in the minutiae. Cyril, nothing must be missed."

***

Liz's body shook involuntarily, her teeth chattered as she tried to control the tremors. As the night hours dragged on, the cold seemed to permeate every bone in her body, regardless of how she wrapped the blanket around herself. Every time her body succumbed to exhaustion and she nodded off, she was soon awakened by the gnawing cold.

The yellow glow from the electric lights filled the recesses of the small, cell-like room as she marked another line on the wall with a shaking hand. She breathed out and watched the air billow in grey clouds, warm breath against cold air. It was at the precise moment when she saw the breath slowly disappearthat she had the first real, clear thought, a mental image came crystal sharp to mind. She could see Cyril Bennett standing in front of her, the vapour from his e-cigarette forming a similar cloud. She closed her eyes and welcomed that moment from her past. It was clear and focussed. She could see his facial features and she smiled to herself in the excitement. She concentrated harder looking beyond Cyril. Yes, she could visualise his office, neat and orderly. She opened her eyes briefly and then closed them again. She could see his shoes, like two black mirrors, his trousers, sharply pressed and then she saw his hands. They were perfectly manicured. A sense of relief flooded her body.

Suddenly, she no longer felt the cold as shementally grasped at these new found images that seemed to appear out of the mists of time. It was like putting together a jigsaw where a few pieces are 'picture up' but the majority are face down. Now, however, more and more were being flipped over in her mind's eye. It was then that she could see Owen and the envelope, she could see his lips moving but she heard no sounds before they broke into a broad smile. She saw her hand move to his head; she struck him. The words filled her head, *French letter.* She said the words over and over again whilst keeping her eyes firmly closed. Next she saw a face that she knew so well, it was Shakti; she was laughing.

"Shakti, dear Shakti!" she said out loud. A warmth of satisfaction bubbled inside her as she scratched three names on the wall above the calendar marks, Cyril, Shakti and Owen. She was now determined to turn more of the puzzle pieces over whilst ensuring that none of her newly found memory was lost. She ran her finger over the freshly scribed marks. It was only then that she realised that she had stopped shaking and no longer felt the cold.

The crashing sound of a door slamming open some way off in the unknown world that existed on the other side of her cell walls, brought an immediate halt to her reminiscence. Shadows moved like black ghosts, elongated and discernible; clearly the many interlinking forms were cast from a number of people, their muffled conversations audible but indecipherable. She strained, trying to catch the odd word but with little success. It was then that she heard the engines, one followed by a second and then a third, trundle just outside her window. A faint whiff of diesel fumes permeated the ill-fitting window frame. Her senses became acute as she listened for the slightest clue as to what was occurring. Maybe this was normal, maybe this was the first day that she was alert enough to appreciate her immediate surroundings and make something of her newfound senses.

Chapter Sixteen

DC Mortimer stood against one of the white boards and watched as a number of colleagues streamed in and found a place to perch. Cyril entered with Margaret Podmore. All eyes followed her, a thirty-something, tall female, with brown hair tied up in a sort of bun. She carried a file under one arm and a brief case. She had more the appearance of a company secretary than a copper.

Cyril didn't sit; he glanced around the room as if taking a mental register. "Morning, and my apologies for this early start." Cyril introduced DI Podmore who nodded to the group but remained silent.

If she had a pound for every time a look of scepticism appeared on colleagues' faces when they became aware that she was from the NCA, she would be retired and living in the Caribbean by now. She took the opportunity to look each in the eye whilst maintaining a smile.

"A good deal of information has come to light over the last few hours. I've got to say a big thanks to Paul who is now doing a second shift, so before he goes home he's going to fill everyone in on the various findings."

Paul explained about the suspect vehicle seen on the dash cam images and the tracking of the van only as far as Pateley Bridge.

"There's a search in the area and a NPAS helicopter (National Police Air Service) will be assisting. Operation Hawk is in full swing in that specific area and the teams have been told to stop and search anything that seems out of the ordinary."

(Operation Hawk is a North Yorkshire Police initiative. Specialist Road Teams, usually comprising two police cars, one unmarked, work together using in- car technology to identify and cross-reference

a suspect vehicle's history and owner details. The cars are linked to the Control Centre in York. This technology allows the successful and swift response to actionable intelligence.)

"We've also asked for unusual heat source detection in the area from the over flights, as it's suspected drug farming may be the reason for the abduction and the murders."

Owen reported on the early morning search revealing that Christina Cameron had travelled to Istanbul under the name of Rosalyn Bruce. He also explained that Istanbul had a connection to an earlier case involving Charles, the suspected murderer. He emphasised that the flight had not been pre-planned as the ticket had only been bought on the day of the flight; the destination, however, might well have been. Interpol had been briefed as had the Turkish Police, but that was all he could say at this stage.

"That could mean the organisation is closing down and shutting up shop," Peg broke into the meeting with a degree of confidence. "It's believed that a missing laptop computer holds the key to finding Liz and that's our number one priority. I suspect it's still hidden or stored where Valerie put it. What we do know is that Charles would like to get his hands on it to either check what secrets it holds, or simply to destroy it. Failing to accomplish that he will simply move away and start up, whatever illegal activities he controls, elsewhere. We also believe that an unknown production company has seen some or all of the data. We're no closer to finding them. We think that Valerie's agent may well more have information than he is divulging, whether this be out of fear we cannot speculate. Certainly he knows what brought about the death of his client. On the other hand, if he were to expose the information, broadcast it and bring it to the attention of the general public anonymously, then he would consider himself safe from harm. It's a gamble. Who knows?" She sat down.

"Peg believes that Liz is still alive," Cyril was only too happy to report. "I'll let her explain."

"From experience there are two reasons, well there can be three reasons to carry out a kidnap. Firstly, to extort money or favours.

We've all heard of cases where girls are kidnapped and kept as sex or domestic slaves. This can be common with people traffickers so in this case cannot be ruled out. However, from the videos we have, Valerie appeared to be a willing participant. Secondly, for revenge; one gang kidnaps and kills and the rival gang does the same, or they kidnap to effectuate a mutual release. Usually, with gangland kidnappings it's the first scenario as I'm sure you're all aware. There's also an increased number of incidents where we see children taken abroad by estranged parents, but this doesn't pertain to Liz's case. The note attached to the spoke found at Liz's apartment is key." She read it out.

'If you perceive yourself to be clever, and smart, there will be someone waiting to outsmart you.'

"It has a definite implication. We now know that the spoke used to break the window and the one found at Liz's apartment match, they're from the wheel found at the scene of the first murder. We know that there has been a number of coincidences running throughout this enquiry. I put it to you that the one person Charles really wants is not DS Graydon, but DCI Bennett. We cannot rule out, either that he intends to demand a swop for Liz or that he is using her as bait to entrap. Should he find Valerie Atkins's laptop in the meantime, that discovery would have a negative effect on the whole nature of the game. The rules would suddenly alter and he would hold an even stronger hand."

Cyril's phone vibrated. He stood and left the room. It was Newby Wiske. They had removed the laptop from store and another video had been received which they were patching through. He returned and walked to the screen at the far end of the room. After Cyril announced the news, there was a deep sense of apprehension as all eyes turned to the screen.

"Anyone who witnessed the first video doesn't need to stay and watch this."

Cyril looked at Owen and then at Shakti. Neither left. Shakti came and stood behind Owen, her hands resting on his shoulders. Cyril found the file and clicked on the start.

"Remember, everyone, that whatever we see here has already happened, it's in the past and we cannot change it."

The video opened, showing Lizsitting alone in the same room as the previous one. The table was to her right and she faced the camera. The grey-white cover suit was marked with a dark stain around the groin and inner thigh area. Shakti involuntarily squeezed Owen's shoulders. He raised a hand and placed it on hers. Each of Liz's legs was taped to those of the chair and her arms, although unseen, were secured behind her. Both her mouth and her eyes were also taped. She seemed alone. The camera focused on her face. She seemed alert her head turning as if listening or trying to sense what was about to happen. It was apparent that she appeared to be testing the strength of her tethers. The cameras then panned to the table before zooming in on two objects, one a bicycle spoke and to its right, a hatpin, its silver, curled head topped with a sapphire-coloured stone. Cyril paused the video.

"That, we believe, is the weapon used to murder both Coulson and Atkins. He looked again. It has all the characteristics of a Charles Horner pin. Note the name, *Charles Horner,* another one of these rapidly increasing coincidences."

The video was re-started. A figure appeared from the side of the screen and apart from a Venetian mask, the man was naked. He picked up the pin from the table and moved behind Liz. He held out both hands in a supplicating manner, the pin in the right. The atmosphere in the Incident Room was tense, as people fidgeted, fearing the worst. Cyril saw Shakti lower her head as the hands on screen moved together in front of Liz's unseeing eyes. Slowly and deliberately, he brought the tip of the pin towards the web-like skin between the finger and thumb of his left hand, before driving the fine steel through the skin. Pomegranate red globules quickly beaded before running and pooling into the now flattened palm. The hand released the elaborately formed and bejewelled crown of the pin, allowing a finger to dip into the human palette of blood.

Cyril stood back a little trying to get a clearer view. The fingertip, acting as a stylus, daubed an eye onto Liz's forehead, a simple circle trapped within an upper and lower line. As the hands drew away and the camera zoomed in on the image, the scene slowly faded to black. There was no sound nor script.

It was a few moments before Cyril moved; all eyes remained focussed on the dark screen.

"Anybody, positives?" Cyril barked, an obvious anger and frustration in his tone as he moved back to the desk.

"Alive and kicking thankfully," Owen said, tapping Shakti on the hand. "He's not our killer, he's right handed."

"I don't think it's about an eye for an eye." Shakti's voice was unsteady. "It's the third eye. The position on the forehead, it's the symbol for the inner eye, an eye that gives us perception beyond ordinary sight, an ability to see what might be."

"I agree, Shakti, it's another sign, a spoke, if you like, a message. It's as if they're informing us that they see the future, that they are controlling the game. What we have to do, ladies and gentlemen, is control that ending. We need to interpret fully the evidence from Cameron's flat, investigate further the dash cam data, pick up anything out of the ordinary from Operation Hawk. We need to interrogate Cooper and Grant, and I mean interrogation and not interview. They might just give us the lead we need. We must also speak to Valerie's brother. The only contact we have to date is through the Wigan Police, at this stage I need more. I've a contact at Wigan so I'll be having a word. Anything and everything should be uplifted to the system." Podmore looked across at Cyril, signalling she had said all that she wanted to say.

"DI Podmore will be here, use her expertise. Owen and Shakti will collect Grant, Ruth is bringing in Cooper whilst Mortimer will be going off to bed with our thanks. After what you've seen this morning, I hope you can sleep."

***

Grant had been unable to view anything on the laptop, the battery was too low and it had not been supplied with a charging lead. He was not happy at all. He read through the note that Valerie had written to her brother, her handwriting was so familiar and he felt a pang of guilt. However, he was also a realist, this information and the promise of a commission was critical to the Agency's future, the prestige would be invaluable even considering the continued risk he ran.

It had to be said that he was more than a little scared. He knew that if whoever had killed Val were to discover that he was now in possession of the information, then his life was in definite danger. Once the data was safely in the hands of the production company, he felt that he could relax. However, he just could not arrive at their doorstep with a computer that, for one, did not work and for two might be totally blank. Until he had seen the content himself, he was in limbo.

***

Ruth knocked at Cooper's door, still choosing to ignore the bell. Surprisingly he was out of bed and even though he looked startled to see her, he did appear a little more human than on the previous visits.

"Bloody hell, Ruth what time do you call this? Problem?"

"You look better than I've seen you in a long time. The eyes are looking a little less like piss holes in snow."

"Thanks for that, bet you say that to all the boys! Now you didn't come all this way to compliment me on my appearance, So…?"

"No problem, John, you're needed at the station to look at some evidence that's come to light.DCI Bennett asked me to call, he needs you to confirm whether the stuff ever belonged to Valerie. Would it be convenient today, now even? I'll run you there and back?" She smiled, trying to appeal to his better nature. "It would help me too." She now lied.

"Of course! Will it take all morning?"

Ruth simply shook her head. She hated compromising her professional position; trust and honesty were key words within the relationships that she had to develop, so this charade did not sit comfortably. True, Cyril had put a few pieces together for him to look at but that in a way seemed to make matters worse.

***

Peg and Smirthwaite checked through the latest Forensic evidence received from Cameron's flat and concentrated on two photographs; one clearly showed her standing with Valerie Atkins in front of a waterwheel, in the other she was at her desk at the Stray Agency.

"Do we know where this was taken?" Peg pointed to the waterwheel.

"That's Wath just outside Pateley Bridge. It's the old mill, now converted into apartments. It's by a pub called The Bridge, I think, Cyril would know the name of the pub. It's a regular tourist stopping point. There must be hundreds of pictures like this one with tourists standing in front of the mill wheel. Give me a minute."

Brian Smirthwaite brought up Google Earth and then Street View.

"Here, look. The mill wheel is huge."

"So we have cars operating in that area now?"

"And the chopper. Anything out of the ordinary will be checked."

***

Cyril had driven into town after receiving a text message from Linda, the overly friendly Receptionist at the local auction house. He leaned through the Reception, opening determined to keep some defence between them.

"Thanks for the text, Linda. Two pins you say and a painting? What's so special?"

"I just happened to be talking to Mr Haveringham, the director of Ilkley's Auction House about your search for Charles Horner pins and he said that they had two in the next sale. A woman brought them in for valuation along with a lovely little painting. What interested me more, and I thought you'd be interested too, was the fact that this lady didn't leave a contact address only a number. That's usually a no, no! Could have been stolen or... anyway, Colin Crompton accepted the items for the Fine Art sale in November, it's on the 25th. I believe you know Colin? Anyway, just thought you should know."

She turned the computer screen round and flicked through all the items photographed in the sale catalogue.

Cyril looked up Haveringham Auction's telephone number.

"Colin Crompton, please!" Cyril looked at Linda and smiled. "Appreciate this, Linda."

Cyril could hear a few voices in the background as Colin was called to the phone.

"Colin, it's Cyril Bennett. Linda tells me you've taken in two Charles Horner pins. What do you know about them?"

Colin explained the story and then described the painting. "Strange woman, Mr Bennett. Allegedly bought it at a car boot sale along with the pins. Everyone says that these days!"

"Colin, I want you to put them in safe keeping. I'm going to have to seize all three items, two might have been used in a serious crime. Have they been exposed to the public?"

"The painting has been hanging in the Director's Office. He usually chooses a picture from each Fine Art sale to hang in his room especially if we use it for the catalogue cover. The Migliaro is particularly attractive. As for the pins, only staff, they were put in the cabinet almost straight away. They've been photographed."

"Seen the catalogue. I'll send someone today for a statement and to collect the items. You wouldn't happen to have any CCTV of our mystery woman would you?"

"I'll check. Probably, providing the system was running on the day. Like many things here, Mr Bennett, it can be a little temperamental."

Cyril turned and thanked Linda. "I owe you a good bottle of red."

"My pleasure I'll hold you to that!"

***

Owen and Shakti escorted Grant through the Reception area and straight to an interview room ensuring that both Cooper and Grant saw each other. Ruth sat with Cooper awaiting Cyril's return. It was a five-minute wait.

He smiled at Ruth and shook Cooper's hand.

"Thanks for coming in Mr Cooper, I'll be just a couple of minutes."

Cyril leaned over the counter and requested collection of the items from the auction house. "Send Nixon and ask him to call me when he gets back." The duty officer then handed him a note left by DI Podmore. "It's urgent, Sir." Cyril read the note and smiled.

He ushered Cooper to another interview room and called for two coffees.

Owen and Shakti were already facing Grant. Peg Podmore was watching both interviews on screen.

"I've told you everything you need to know, I know nothing more."

"The railway station cameras have been very helpful to you, Mr Grant. CCTV corroborated your story for last Friday. They can, however, be a double-edged sword." Owen left it there and enjoyed watching Grant's confused facial contortions.

"Sorry, I don't know what you're talking about."

"Has your car been stolen?"

"What? Has it bloody hell, you parked behind it when you invited me here."

"Why were you travelling in your car along the East Lancashire Road, the A580, yesterday evening? Seems a long way to go for a brief visit. According to our records, your car was then seen returning forty minutes later. Go for a pie? After all, Wigan's famous for that culinary delight."

Grant's face was now scarlet, the tell tale sweat marks were growing ever more noticeable.

Owen took delight in leaning over the table and formally cautioning Grant. "Just to make sure, Mr Grant, that you're in no doubt as to the serious trouble you might be in, let me remind you that a senior police officer has been missing for four days and we feel that you're withholding vital information that may be obstructing her recovery. At the moment we believe she's still alive. However, should those circumstances change and we find that the information you're withholding could have…" Owen did not continue.

Peg Podmore left the surveillance area after handing a memory stick to the other officer. "On my signal."

She knocked before entering the interview room. Owen looked round.

"May I ask the suspect a question, DS Owen?"

The word *suspect* made Grant sit up straight. "I've told you everything I know!"

"Before you say anything else, may I remind you that you're under oath. You've been informed that this interview is being filmed and recorded for your sake as well as ours." She smiled at him. Owen shivered; she was like a snake eyeing its prey. "I want you to look at that screen." She lifted her hand.

Grant didn't immediately recognise the scene, it was only when he saw himself appear at the glass doors, the German Shepherd and the caretaker that his worst fears were confirmed. Podmore lifted her hand for the second time and the video stopped.

"Now, humour me, Mr Grant. What did you sign for? What exactly was in the package? It wouldn't be a laptop would it by any chance?"

Grant shook his head but then nodded.

"I need a verbal answer, Mr Grant. Is that your signature?"

"Yes."

"Now, Mr Grant, you are in extremely serious trouble. We're looking at possibly murder or an accessory to murder. Shall we start at the beginning?"

Owen looked at Shakti and smiled. Podmore certainly was impressive.

***

Cooper looked at the three items and confirmed that two, as far as he was aware, belonged to Val, the third he was unsure of.

"Thanks, Mr Cooper." Cooper started to stand. "Just one more thing."

Cooper smiled and sat down.

"Can you tell me why Frederick Grant, your partner's agent, should meet up with her brother, to collect something from him, in fact?"

Cooper's whole demeanour changed, he suddenly became more rigid.

"I can see there's awareness in your eyes. Before we do the next bit…" Cyril cautioned him. "It's serious now. This information, Mr Cooper, has only just come to light, I've not yet seen it."

He waved his hand and the screen on the far wall lit up. The footage of Grant arriving at the school Reception showed. When it finished, Cyril turned to him.

"What did Mr Grant collect? I know that you know."

It took all of thirty minutes for Cooper to explain the call from James Atkins, Grant's belief that getting Val's laptop to him would be a testimonial to Val's legacy and also the possibility of royalties. It had to be said that he cut a dejected figure.

***

The police car gradually brought the box van to a halt as the unmarked car closed tightly behind. It also closed Red Brae Bank. The passenger in the van threw open the door and jumped the fence before running into thick woodland. The driver tried to do the same but was caught on the barbed wire fence. It had just been a routine stop, the vehicle was licensed to a rental firm based in Halifax. The bolting occupants confirmed that the stop was justified. When they rolled up the rear shutter door the officers were in absolutely no doubt. Eight, young, dark-skinned females were huddled in the far end of the van accompanied by sixteen large bags of what appeared to be drugs.

One of the officers moved the vehicle off the road onto a farm gate entrance before calling for back up.

***

Within fifteen minutes Grant had told them everything. He had genuinely believed the laptop to be lost until Cooper had received the call from Val's brother. Neither Shakti nor Owen was convinced that he was risking everything to redress the wrong that Valerie had suffered as a result of the first documentary. The fact that he had kept valuable intelligence from the police might well have put himself, Cooper and Liz in harm's way. There would, they assured him, be serious consequences.

Owen escorted Grant to collect the laptop and within the hour the computer was on its way to Newby Wiske. Grant, however, was sitting in a cell and so too was Cooper.

***

The three items collected from the Ilkley Auction House had been couriered directly to Forensics and the statement was sitting on Cyril's desk along with a disc. He collected them and went into the Incident Room.

"Shakti, put this on, footage of our mystery car boot lady."

Within seconds Cyril identified the woman as Cameron.

"Her prints will be all over the painting and the pins. If they contain traces of DNA from Atkins and Coulson, we might have our murder weapons. How deeply is Grant involved in all of this, if at all? Or was Cameron planted at the Stray Agency to help discover just what Atkins was up to? Did anyone interview the previous secretary?"

Cyril received blank faces as Owen checked through HOLMES.

"Paula Baker. No, she left before both murders, a good three months. Cameron's placement started mid August so she had time to find out what was going on. She was planted there. I'll organise an interview with Miss Baker."

Peg Podmore entered. "Cyril, Met Police has sent a report after interviewing the manager of Revelations, the production company that preliminarily commissioned the documentary, 'Modern Farming Today'. They confirmed that that was the working title. They saw the evidence on a laptop and Valerie Atkins was, according to their staff, exceptionally convincing and professional. Its evidence covered people trafficking, importing drugs and cannabis production within the rural community of North Yorkshire. They were not allowed to keep the images until a formal contract had been signed. Grant had been down in London the day Liz was taken. They report that he was there to plead for more time. Allegedly, Valerie had suffered a bout of depression and he had played the medical card. Generously, they extended the deadline by a week. Nobody was aware that Valerie had been murdered. Unbelievably, since knowing the consequences of her investigation and the material held, they are now keen to extend the deadline indefinitely and are happy to sign an open contract. Mercenary bastards!"

She dropped the report in front of Cyril. "It'll be on there shortly, all the names etc." She pointed to the computer in front of Owen.

Chapter Seventeen

Charles sat on the floor opposite the makeshift bed. Liz was propped in the corner, the rough blanket cocooning her. He looked at the chain that appeared out from the side of the blanket before rising to the ring on the wall; a steel umbilical cord. He then noticed the scratchings. There were now four vertical lines crossed through, a tally of time. It was the name Cyril on which he focussed.

He stood and moved over to the wall, stretching out the nail-varnished index finger before tracing the word. Each time he followed the letters, he applied more force until the finely manicured nail began to scratch and erase the lettering.

Liz, sensing someone was close, barely opened her eyes; she remained motionless and afraid. Charles moved away, returning to the far end of the cell. He stared at the damaged varnish before smoothing the nail's now rough edge with his other hand.

"Bitch! Bitch!" she heard him whisper. "I know you can hear me, I saw your eyes open and then close. You can stop this pretence otherwise I'll give you something that will make you sit up."

Liz opened her eyes and focused on the man sitting opposite, his crossed legs, his bleach blonde hair seemed totally incongruous with his muscular build.

"We haven't been formally introduced, even though, my dear, I guess you could say that I know you intimately." He lifted his head and stared back at her. The endless depth to that stare made the hairs on her neck and arms tingle. "Don't worry, ladies are not on my preferred menu."

Liz immediately heard alarm bells ring in her head. The fact that he was here, facing her in plain sight, telling her who he was, made her shudder. Why would he suddenly allow her to see him, know him? She instantly felt nauseous.

"It's all Bennett's fault, your Cyril!" He pointed to the mark where she'd scratched his name and she noticed that it had been totally defaced. "We had a good business, steady, lucrative, bringing no harm to anyone. Years we ran it, like clockwork, tick, tock, tick, tock. And then along comes Cyril Bloody Bennett!"

Liz shuffled uncomfortably on the bed, rattling the chain as she tightened the grip around her legs.

Charles took from his pocket what appeared to be a piece of broken glass. He rolled it along the floor until it ricocheted off the side of the bucket before coming to rest between them.

"You'll not know what that is. No, you'll think it's a piece of worthless glass, a trinket, but then you don't know much do you DS Graydon? In fact you know fuck all. That..." he pointed to the glass almost hidden in the dirt, "that little piece of carbon is what's known as a rough diamond. Some people called them blood diamonds. How many people died extracting these? It doesn't matter, the rebels controlled the diamonds and you were either with them or you were rendered armless." Charles laughed. "Armless get it? Fuck, girl you know nothing. Christ if you didn't join the rebels they removed your hands or arms so you couldn't dig for stones or fight against them. Anyway, parents were happy to get their daughters out of the country and we offered that service for small pouches of these. They believed their girls were going to help in family homes in Europe, safely away from the rapists and murdering youths of Sierra Leone. In some ways that was true but in others, it was from a frying pan into a fire!"

Liz took a deep breath, angered both by his arrogance and her weakness.

"Child prostitution, pornography, drug addiction, that's what you gave them, not the promise of a better life!" Liz suddenly felt outrage overtake her fear. She had seen what traffickers did to young lives.

Charles was startled by the anger in her words. "You judge me too soon, we gave them something that they and their parents didn't have and couldn't hope ever to have."

"Don't you lecture me, don't you dare tell me you gave them hope! You sit there as if you were some kind of charity, some kind of benevolent god and saviour. I've seen what happens to these children, it's happening all over Europe right now. People are taking advantage of those in dire need of assistance, desperate people who trust the words of those who appear to be in a position to help. All too sadly, they fail to comprehend the one human frailty that's ever present and that's greed, Charles, greed. Avarice, in the eyes of many, including myself, is a sin. Think what good you could have done!"

Where this courage had come from she would never know, but she was not one to listen to bullshit no matter how tight a corner she was in. Whatever she said now would not change the outcome of her predicament, maybe it would accelerate whatever end she faced.

"Good? I've never been good, ever in my entire life. You've no idea what being sinful has brought me."

"Trinkets that are for the here and now, it's material wealth, not spiritual. It has no value other than to those who seek the same, the greedy and the selfish. You'll never take them with you. Come the day, you'll have exactly the same possessions as me, only you'll have the crippling burden of guilt. I despise what you've done to those human beings before me and I despise what you're doing to me. You'll never get me to bend or bow to you no matter how much you frighten me. Yes, you do frighten me, you've hurt me and done whatever else to me. You might break me physically but you'll never change the Liz that's in here."

Charles clenched his fists and felt the frustration build inside. "Bennett will bend, he'll feel the crippling burden of guilt and he'll carry it with him for ever. He will come and I'll crush him."

He smashed a fist into the palm of his hand before standing to collect the diamond. He held it between a finger and thumb admiring the refracted coloured light.

"I'm not greedy." He tossed the gem into the bucket. "I'm no different from the High Street entrepreneur. I'm a businessman, I give people what they want and I take a fee, there's no difference. And now, goody two shoes, they're queuing along the African coast, ready to be picked like ripe apples. Life has got so much easier. No matter what you say or what you do, it will never stop. Business is blooming, bitch!" He left the room slamming the door.

Hearing those few words, Liz knew that her life would never be the same again. The nausea returned and she moved quickly to the bucket and vomited.

Chapter Eighteen

Cyril and Shakti looked at the images of the girls, as they had been taken from the van.

"We're getting warmer, Shakti. I wonder which one of those we saw on the video? It also looks as though we have the source of Valerie's habit. The driver's said nothing and the accomplice is still at large. Dogs and helicopter are searching. He shouldn't get far."

The late afternoon was busy but there had still been no contact with the missing passenger from the van. The girls had been interviewed but very little was known of their location, but a vital clue surfaced in that they had not been travelling. They gave a detailed description of their arrival in England including quite a graphic description of a journey in a small boat and how they had been extremely wet, hungry and cold. Two also described being sexually abused. They described with great accuracy the room and the film set up.

"I want a full house to house of Pateley Bridge tomorrow, particularly any garages or industrial units. If that brings nothing, we'll increase the sweep to include the outlying farms."

All the while the cost of the operation was weighing heavily on Cyril's mind. He would need to seek support from a higher level.

He was just passing the Reception counter at the building's entrance when the phone rang; the duty officer answered as he watched Cyril pass. He immediately dropped the receiver and dashed after him. Cyril returned mumbling under his breath that he should dig a bloody tunnel to escape.

"Bennett."

"It's Peg. Thought you'd like to know that the laptop Grant collected was blank apart from Valerie's videos. He wouldn't have been able to extract those as they were heavily encrypted. Someone's cleared it or saved it and cleared it. I've been in touch with Wigan and James Atkins isn't at school nor at home. Wasn't in work today; he rang in sick at 07:55. The shits apparently."

"Check for his car."

"It's at his house. Neighbours say it hasn't moved all day. Nobody has seen him."

"See if anyone holds a spare key and get them to take a look, if not put a watch on him. I'll organise a warrant. How did Owen go on with Paula Baker?"

"He said he'd call if there's anything to report. Have a good evening."

"And you, don't work too hard. Remember very early start again tomorrow."

Peg had no intention of leaving, there were one or two loose ends she had to look into, besides a hotel room held little attraction. She immediately rang The Jeffrey's building to chase up the DNA on the pins and painting seized from the Ilkley Auction House. As suspected, the painting contained Christina Cameron's prints but the pins held the DNA of both Coulson and Valerie Atkins; brain tissue traces were detected on both as well as vitreous humour on one. They now had a direct link with the murder weapons and Cameron.

Peg was sitting next to Paul Mortimer who had just returned on shift. Owen came into the Incident Room. He tossed his car keys onto the table and went for a drink.

He returned to the room stirring the coffee, allowing the contents to dribble down the sides before placing the mug on the table. A small, brown reservoir collected around the base.

"It's right what it says on this mug, *Harrogate* and *Crime.* Never seem to see much of the other things marked, like *Art* and *Festivals.* I could do with going to a bloody good festival." He stopped stirring and the spillage stopped.

"Well, do you bring tidings of great joy?"

"Where's Flash?"

"Governors' Meeting at the local Primary School and then he's seeing Julie. He said something about returning some property he'd borrowed."

Owen just smiled and winked. "Right!"

"Well, she didn't jump she was pushed!" He slurped his coffee. "Paula Baker. She was never pregnant. She was shagging Grant but was never... anyway, it appears that she had a visit from a very persuasive gentleman who recommended she leave. The pregnancy was all contrived."

"The gentleman who paid her a visit?"

"Large, blonde. Offered her money, a year's salary and support with the story. She did very well out of it, Grant turned over ten grand for her to terminate what wasn't there. Little did he know he was about to introduce a cuckoo as well as a new squeeze into his office!"

Peg moved away from the table. "Cyril was right, they, Cameron and Charles knew that Valerie was onto something from the social media links with Coulson. You can see why the police keep a very close eye on social media as the potential for crime is massive. By the way, Owen, Grant's been duped again. The laptop he collected from Valerie's brother had been cleaned. Seems James Atkins has done a runner too unless, of course, Charles has got to him first."

Owen slurped the dregs from the bottom of his mug. "Could never quite understand that relationship. She hated him, he hated her, he even stated that he wouldn't come to the funeral, hated Cooper for something that occurred at school. Hated his parents. Doesn't make sense to me and then she goes and leaves the most valuable item..."

"And the most dangerous don't forget."

"Yes, there is that. You don't think she's deliberately put him in harm's way, do you?"

"Retribution! Remember, Owen, revenge is best served cold. After all, she's well and truly cold. You should also know, murder weapons are the two Charles Horner pins, DNA. Clever to leave them in the auction, another month and they could have gone anywhere."

***

Cyril crossed Skipton Road before taking the footpath. His scarf was wrapped high around his neck as a northerly breeze brought what seemed an early winter chill. He could see Julie's apartment across the short patch of The Stray. He rang the bell and Julie appeared in the bay window. She smiled.

He stumbled in as the door automatically unlocked. He felt the immediate welcoming warmth against his cold face. What a last few days! He just needed an hour of reality and he would be thinking straight again.

As he entered Julie's apartment, he immediately saw the glass of whiskey on the coffee table alongside the two hatpin boxes.

"Thought you'd need the cockles of your heart warming, DCI Bennett." She smiled and moved across to kiss him. "You poor creature, your nose is like ice."

She took his coat.

"What news? Shop talk is most definitely allowed this evening."

Cyril went through the whole case as she topped up his glass and fed him slices of pizza.

"You obviously pissed this Charles guy off pretty badly but you didn't arrest him."

"Never ever saw him, a ghost as far as we were concerned."

"So why, if he's running a business in this country again, commit crimes that are so, so, in your face for want of a better description?"

"They're committed to drawing me in. DI Peg Podmore from NCA believes he's going to demand a swap, me for Liz. I'm happy for that to happen but whether the powers that be will agree is another matter. It's out of my hands. Anyway we're crossing bridges before we can even see the rivers."

"Why would Atkins post a laptop to her brother, a brother she'd not seen for ages, didn't communicate with, siblings who supposedly didn't like each other? Christ, Cyril, you said that she even lived with the bloke who drove her brother away. Now if I'd been her brother, that would have pissed me off, believe me! There's something called family loyalty."

Cyril sipped the whiskey and slipped his feet onto the coffee table.

"I'm getting too old for this, Julie. I've just got to get Liz back. Tomorrow there'll be a mass of coppers stomping throughout Pateley Bridge but we've no guarantee she's anywhere near. The group of illegals stopped today may have been the last tranche."

Cyril glanced across at Julie who was pacing the far end of the room, deep in thought.

"Valerie lost a sister when she was younger, hit and run, I think you said when we last spoke."

"That's right. James was with them: being the oldest he was responsible for looking after them. Driver was never found. Mother reported that he became quite introverted after the accident, cold like his father, I believe she said."

"Let me run this past you Cyril, a woman's perspective. Imagine that his reluctance, his introverted behaviour was not a feeling of guilt for his failure to look after his sister, but a guilt for not telling the truth, a truth that covered up for his sister."

Cyril flicked his feet back to the carpet and sat up.

"Let's imagine that Valerie was jealous of her younger sister, that she was the one responsible. Let's imagine that they were by the side of the busy road and she was holding hands with Jennifer and as they were about to cross, Valerie pushed Jennifer into the side of a passing car by accident or a deliberate act. Witnessed only by her brother, a brother who should also have been holding Jennifer's hand. Imagine the mental turmoil, the maelstrom of emotional conflict. He couldn't tell the truth. Valerie probably had it already worked out, even at her young age. That's why James was so morally judgemental about Cooper's cheating."

"So why would his mother refer to him as cold like his dad?"

"Look, Cyril, this is all hypothetical. The only person to alleviate some of the guilt was his father, when they were fishing or chatting or mending his bike, I don't know. But at some stage the lie or should we say the truth was shared. A burden shared is a burden halved."

"So why not hand in the laptop, wash his hands of the whole thing? He seemed up until that point to have his life together."

"To show Cooper's immoral nature, to expose him for what he was and is. Same with Grant, he wanted to set the record straight."

"So why go missing, why keep the data that everyone's chasing?"

"He's denying his sister. He's eventually paying her back. If Grant had received the information, there's a strong likelihood that the recognition she would receive posthumously would have been more than she received throughout her career. James knew just what that meant to her so he pulled the plug. She gave him the chance; she tried to right her wrong. It was like saying to him after all these years, you do what's right, James."

"The workings of the female mind!" He stood and stretched. "Need to get back. Thanks, Julie."

"You're not walking." She picked up the phone and dialled for a taxi.

***

Cyril went directly to the Incident Room. He checked the boards and the latest information, trying to get up to speed. Peg was in a far corner.

"Just the lady I wanted to see. Have you eaten?"

"Showered, changed and feasted." She brought her nose to her armpit and sniffed loudly. "Can't you tell?"

Cyril chuckled. "The delicate smell of roses!"

She simply smiled but what she really wanted to reply was, *men*!

Perching on the edge of one of the tables, he took her through Julie's theory. She rejected none of it.

"Intuition, Cyril. She's made some interesting points that certainly help to make sense of things, but with Valerie's death died the truth." She paused. "I've had a word with my boss and he's organised more troops from afar for tomorrow's search. We'll need them!"

His phone rang. "Bennett."

Cyril started to wave his hand at the large screen signalling that he wanted it made ready. Peg moved quickly and switched it on.

"There's a new video, arrived fifteen minutes ago. Just get Mortimer in here! Is Owen about?"

"Wouldn't stay home, went to shower, change and is back, armed with a large pork pie and crisps. As I say I've eaten."

"Please get him in here too."

Within seconds, the mood in the room had changed, the atmosphere seemed thick and viscous. Butterflies jumped in Cyril's stomach and he felt suddenly weak. He was not a religious man but he found himself closing his eyes and saying a few words in the hope that Liz was still alive.

Owen, Mortimer and Peg came into the room.

"I sent Shakti home. She protested but she went," Owen said as he sat next to Cyril. They both took a deep breath before starting the video.

The room and table were familiar, it was as if nothing had changed. Liz was still in the same place, strapped and bound, her eyes blindfolded with tape, her legs strapped; the same red-brown stain still visible. The camera focussed solely on her. They watched as she moved her head from side to side as if trying to glean any clues as to her location; it was a pitiful spectacle. Owen pointed to the screen, demanding that they look at her right breast. Cyril paused the video. Protruding from the paper coverall was the elaborate, jewelled head of a Charles Horner pin. The opposite end could be seen exposed.

"It looks as if the pin has been attached as a brooch. There's no blood, it's through the cover not through Liz, thankfully."

The video was restarted and the camera panned away from Liz, revealing more of the table. Sitting open was a laptop, the screen looked hazy until the camera zoomed in. Prominent on the home page was a photograph of Valerie and her friends taken at some time in Harrogate. Cyril paused it again.

"Those icons are displayed in exactly the same sequence as we saw on the laptop collected from Dan Rowney. All we had was the videos," Cyril observed.

He then pressed play. A hand moved into shot and the mouse moved the arrow to one of the icons and opened the file. Valerie Atkins's face filled the screen as she whispered to the hand-held phone camera. She then allowed the camera to pan around. Rows of cannabis plants were brightly visible under high intensity lights. The screen went back to the home page before another file was opened. Again Valerie was talking quietly to camera, her voice a little shaky. She turned the camera again to show a group of young girls some white and some coloured, huddling naked in the corner of a room. Each carried a Venetian-style mask. Again the screen went dark.

The camera panned away again revealing Liz, only this time she had a sheet of paper attached to her chest by the pin and her head was down. There no longer seemed to be any awareness. The camera zoomed in again showing only the hand-written message:

Game, set and match, Bennett.
Goodbye,
Charles.

The screen went dark.

As before, nothing was said. They were each momentarily lost in their thoughts.

"Peg, anything on James Atkins?"

"As yet, nothing."

"Seems strange that the only possible link with Valerie Atkins's computer has disappeared at the same time it turns up in Charles's hands. There are two possibilities; Charles discovered that he had it and therefore Atkins is no longer with us or he's involved and has been since receiving the laptop. Who knows what's on it, but I bet it gave a clue as to the location of the farm if the title of the project is to be believed. Brave man who approaches the lion's den and shoves in a stick like young Albert."

Owen turned to look at Cyril. "Who the hell's young Albert?"

"With his stick with a horse's head handle he shoved it in Wallace's ear! Never mind you're too young, Owen, just too young. Dangerous game. He may now not cut and run. He'll close down, change the place, probably stash all the equipment or bury it, but now he feels he's safe. The 'Goodbye' is a sham. If he's there, if he's in the area, we'll find him or his henchmen tomorrow."

***

Carla Bonhomme moved the chair away from the table and tidied the studio. She was still a little shaken by what she had witnessed and her hand shook slightly. She'd experienced many things in her time, particularly since working specifically for Charles. The pornography was nothing now, it was easy, mechanical; she could blank that, forget it and move on. Besides no one died in the making of the videos. The promotional sales' packages that she produced were pure marketing, she actually enjoyed the creative side and the girls were often willing participants. Fancy dresses and luxury locations filled the girls' minds with an expectation that, in most cases, proved totally false. After all, prostitution was just that, one of the world's oldest professions; even so, it didn't prevent her from feeling sorry for some of the young and immature girls. Tonight's filming had been downright callous and sadistically cruel.

She moved across the yard to the main house. A single, high-powered spot light came on as she triggered the sensor. The light flooded the cobbles and illuminated surrounding walls. As she entered, she heard one of the girls singing in a language that she didn't understand, soft and melodic, adding a strange ambivalence to the Yorkshire farmhouse that had witnessed murder and depravity. At least there was one person with some hope, whether that hope were misplaced was not for her to judge. Who knew what hell those girls had experienced in their young lives.

The rooms were now almost empty of the luxuries that Charles so enjoyed. There were only two girls left, both entrusted with cleaning and feeding the skeleton staff that remained.

Charles had been angry at the loss of the van, the girls and particularly the drugs. He had shown little charity to the only person who had managed to flee the police; returning to the farm was considered irresponsible, as far a Charles was concerned. He would not do it again.

Carla rested her hands on the oak table and stared at the brown stain; she had heard the graphic details and knew that it was all that remained of Dan's life-blood. Her hands still shook slightly as she lifted them before clamping them together and then she made her decision. She went to her room. Having ensured that the video had been sent to the police-held laptop, Charles had left the farmhouse. She did not have the worry of seeing him or more to the point, his seeing her. She checked her watch; it was a quarter to midnight. She packed the bare essentials but double-checked that she had the three memory cards. She slipped them inside a condom and tied it. To be caught with them would prove to be a costly and no doubt very painful mistake. Initially, she contemplated swallowing the package but then decided she might need to retrieve and dispose of it quickly soshe inserted it into her vagina. She collected another sweater and a travel rug and stuffed them into a small rucksack before going to the kitchen. She collected a lump of cheese and a bottle of water; it was going to be a long, cold night. It was time to go.

The courtyard would remain in darkness and would continue to do so until the sensor detected movement within its range.

Carla worked her way round the periphery, keeping as far as possible from the sleeping light before exiting on to the long, tree-lined farm track that led to the road. She had escaped and she relaxed briefly. She glanced at the star-filled-sky as her breath streamed in clouds. She pulled her coat tighter and lifted the small rucksack onto her shoulder. There was going to be another frost.

Her eyes slowly grew accustomed to the dark as she hugged the edge of the track. The gravel was sharp and uncomfortable against the soles of her shoes. It was when she rounded the bend that her heart missed a beat.

***

It was Peg who had decided to move early on the search of James Atkins's house, purely out of concern for his welfare. It had proved a wise and professional decision. The house had been found tidy and organised. On the kitchen work surface they had been left a collection of scrapbooks and personal correspondence. Each item had been photographed and sent to Harrogate. Peg and Shakti read through them.

The news cuttings of the accident were upsetting, three children had left home for some fun at a local playground but only two returned, Jennifer, the youngest, was reported as being struck by a hit and run driver. Each cutting was carefully stuck in the book. However, the contents of the accompanying exercise book contradicted the reports, adding a greater degree of detail.

They sat and read the evidence. Being the oldest, James had been given money to buy sweets for the three of them. Apparently, there had always been a good deal of sibling rivalry, falling out and jealousy between the girls, usually because Valerie was envious of her spoiled, younger sister. She knew that their father doted on her, he called her his little Poppet but he never had a pet name for Valerie. According to James, after leaving the playground they called in for sweets. On the way home, Valerie had eaten hers and was bullying Jennifer for some of hers. They started to squabble over the bag and it was then that Valerie had pushed Jennifer off the kerb and into the path of a passing car.

"According to this and obviously it's been written much later, the driver neither saw nor heard the child make contact."

'*I was frightened. Being the oldest, I felt responsible and when the ambulance and the police arrived, the severity of the situation instigated the cover up. A while later, having summoned enough courage, I mentioned it to father who simply beat me and continued to do so over the slightest misdemeanour. He also started drinking heavily, mother put it down solely to the death of his daughter but that was my fault too.*'

Shakti brought two coffees and they both stretched.

"Some kids would be just fine without parents!"

They continued to read.

'*Valerie had initially welcomed the lies, in fact, she pleaded with me not to say what had really happened. As she grew older, she used the fabricated story to serve her own ends. I grew to loathe my sister, her insecurities and her jealousy, the blackmail and her vindictive personality. The only time I felt free was when I was away at university. On my return, I settled down, I'd found a place of my own and she was off to university herself. However, when she returned, I was teaching in Harrogate. She began to encroach again, befriending and living with my best mate. She'd be jealous if John came for a drink. I believe she was behind his cheating of the marking system; she was desperate that he should be promoted above me. I knew then that she was doing drugs, a habit from her student days. There were also rumours of her being sexually promiscuous. I warned John but obviously she had the ability to make him see differently. They say that love is blind.*'

Peg turned to Shakti, "It's all very matter of fact, and there's a steeliness to his writing, a total lack of emotion. Do you sense it?"

Shakti nodded.

'*Her death.*' The word had been crossed through and replaced with '*murder*'. *Her murder wasn't a surprise to me. She played close to the edge. The documentaries she produced, the interviews, direct and frank. Some might say hard-hitting but there was more. So when the laptop arrived and the note, I thought she was setting me up for a fall. I wondered who else knew that I had it. I could see a lot of what was on the drive. Some files were password protected and I couldn't see them but she'd given me the password for many. It was on seeing those that I realised the serious game she was playing. She was up to her neck.*

I downloaded and kept the data before cleaning what I could from the hard drive. You know the rest. The note from Valerie pleaded with me not to let Grant have the data. I called John, to tell him I had the laptop. Up until that point, he was totally innocent, he knew nothing. I think that she tried to trick me even in death. She knew that I would do the exact opposite of her request which was to send it to Grant.

'*What I must do now is think, give myself time to think.*'

"Cyril was nearly right with his theory on the Atkins," Shakti proclaimed.

"It was his pathologist girl friend who came up with that. Takes a woman, Shakti, takes a woman!"

***

The dark figure stood, stock still, almost in the centre of the driveway.

"Charles. Is that you?"

For a moment there was silence.

"Carla, taking the air? Now where might you be going on such a nippy night, eh?" His voice was camp.

"I thought that you'd…"

She didn't finish her sentence. He started to move towards her.

"Tell Uncle Charlie where you thought he'd gone."

Chapter Nineteen

The dawn was slow to break as Cyril and Owen sat in the car park on the edge of Pateley Bridge, nursing two polystyrene coffee cups. Three coaches were parked regimentally straight, four police vans and a large command trailer with its large antennae positioned along one corner of the unit had been organised. A generator hummed a short distance away. As well as two CSI vehicles, there was even a small catering van positioned centrally, its own generator adding to the early morning chorus.

"She's got to be here, Owen, in this area or we've bloody lost her."

The two old fashioned, iron lamps positioned on either side of the car park gates went off as the sky lightened even more. A grey, ethereal mist seemed to cling to the river like a protective blanket as it folded over the car park walls.

Officers climbed out of the coaches and the two dog teams mustered, a mass of hot breath and excitement. It was then that Cyril noticed the limp sign hanging loose and torn on the cricket pitch fence, *Nidderdale Show, September 18th*. He thought of Liz and what they had been doing just over a month ago. That short time had taken its toll on the sign and Cyril felt just as weather worn.

All the officers had their instructions and the Command trailer would co-ordinate in-coming information. One mini bus remained closed; it contained the Specialist Firearms' Officers. They would remain there unless they were called upon.

Cyril's phone rang. "Bennett."

The group of police moved away from the car park, crossed the bridge before spreading out through Pateley Bridge. Cyril watched as he listened to Pegrelay the findings from James Atkins's house. It brought a smile to his face as she commented that Julie was pretty much on the money with her theory. The thought of Julie at that moment lifted his spirits a little. He went across to the control unit.

It was 11:51 when the call came in. A fisherman, higher up the valley, just below Wath had reported what he believed to be a body.

"Says here, Sir, that it's in the middle of a field, thought it was a scarecrow but then there's no crops. It wasn't there two days ago."

Cyril's heart fluttered. "Exact location?"

"Best take Lower Wath Road, you'll be closer to the crime scene."

Cyril and Owen, followed by one of the dog vans, headed along the advised route until they saw the sign for The Farmer's Arms turning right over a narrow bridge, they crossed the River Nidd, the waterway was a mere two metres across.

"Just after the bridge on the right there should be a wooden footbridge," Owen instructed and on cue it appeared and so did the scarecrow. Ironically a crow was sitting on its left shoulder and two others were on the floor, occasionally flying up to peck at the face.

Owen was about to leave the car when Cyril put his hand on his arm. "It could be Liz so prepare yourself for that."

Owen dropped his head and nodded.

"Let the dog do its job first, another ten minutes can't harm her now." Cyril lowered the window and called for the dog handler to check the area.

A stream fed into the Nidd that ran just over and below the wall, the reason for the footbridge. A cushion of mist still clung to the water's surface. The dog's lead extended as it initially sniffed around the crucifixion-like figure before turning and walking down to the stream. Once at the small confluence, it continued across; it checked sniffing, its nose high once over the other side as it began to climb the banking. The handler could see the grass had been recently crushed. The dog moved to the left behind the small, stone bus shelter before making its way to the front where the entrance was situated. It sat momentarily before working the parking area. It returned and sat again in the same spot.

Cyril and Owen crossed the stone bridge and stood on the road looking at the dog and its handler.

"The body was probably moved from here and then down the bank there, across and up the stream before dumping it. I'd suggest more that one trip but only one person. There should be prints in the soft soil on the water's edge."

Owen called for Scene of Crimes and began taping off the area as Cyril called for the Police Pathologist.

"When you've done that, Owen, go up to The Farmer's Arms. I want a list of everyone who was in the pub last night and those there now. Nobody leaves. Close the road there with the car and put the van up by the hotel." Cyril then slipped on a pair of nitrile gloves and overshoes before crossing the footbridge.

The corpse was taped to a makeshift cross that had been forced into the soft ground; the cross-member ran behind her back and then across her forearms. Tape ran under her armpits circling the timber which held her securely. Cyril did not need to check for signs of life, the signs of death were abundantly clear; her neck was broken. A thin layer of white ice adorned her hair and the edge of her clothing; birds had already taken the eyes and had started on the tongue. She had been there a few hours.

"So who on earth are you, young lady, and what did you do to deserve this?"

He moved back across the wooden footbridge, inhaling deeply on his e-cigarette. Strangely, all he felt was relief, no sadness for the young woman, just relief that it was not Liz hung out for the birds. "Scarecrow indeed!" he mumbled as he waited for Forensics. It would be another forty minutes before the Pathologist arrived.

***

Peg had organised distribution of James Atkins's details to the local news agencies and images were now circulating on social media. A number of people had called to inform the police that he was a teacher but what did they expect, all information was welcomed.

To Peg, it all seemed too clinical, too cut and dried. Was he really denying Val her posthumous moment of glory? It was possible or had it all been an elaborate set up? Had somebody got to him first, his body disposed of, clinical and clean, leaving a wake that was purely credible? She would await the rest of the evidence from the house. Had he been taken, there would be clear evidence, clear signs of a struggle. Strangely, there was no report of a personal computer in the house. She rang her contact, a DS Rebecca Pugh, at Wigan Police.

"Peg, we've checked, locker at school, store room, anywhere that James Atkins had access to, we've checked, and before you ask we've chatted with the school's IT staff. Believe me they weren't too happy being woken at five thirty! Listen, we know how much this means but it also means a great deal to us too and we're pulling out all the stops. If we find anything you'll be the second to know… I'll be first!"

***

By the time Cyril arrived at the country hotel and pub, Owen had almost completed the lists and corresponding addresses. Cyril showed his warrant card to the manager.

"Thanks for your co-operation. People should be able to leave using the top road as soon as the body has been removed. I take it from DS Owen that nobody heard or saw anything out of the ordinary?"

The manager shook his head. "Quiet as the grave normally. Sorry! Dead quie…," he paused, realising the inappropriate nature of his comments. "Nothing goes on usually. I think I need a coffee, you Detective Chief Inspector?"

Cyril smiled. "Black, no sugar, thanks. Nippy out there this morning!" He then popped to the toilet; too much coffee, too much water and too early a start.

Within three hours the area was clear and by four in the afternoon the door to door checks were complete. Being such a small community, there was very little intelligence gleaned. The coaches pulled out of the car park one after the other. They would return the next day for a broader search of the outlying area using smaller vehicles and motorcycles.

Cyril walked past the catering vehicle as the side screens were in the process of being closed. The generator was still thumping gently, its job nearly complete. It sounded as weary as he. The Command unit was brightly lit and was now connected to mains' electricity. He entered and the warmth embraced him.

A number of officers was staring at the computer screens adding the minutest pieces of information. Owen looked up as Cyril entered.

DI Podmore rang. "There's a match with a print taken from the painting that was at the Ilkley Auction House. It's been linked to a John Michael Collins, courtesy of our colleagues in Europol. Prints and DNA profile taken regarding a GBH case eight years ago. He was bailed but disappeared, no known whereabouts. Believed to be living in Menton, South of France. No trace of his leaving France, or arriving here for that matter. He obviously moves using false names and documentation We have an old photograph. Owen passed the image to Cyril. We think now he's blonde!"

"Little by little, Owen we're nibbling away. Come on and get your coat. Two pints of Black Sheep are awaiting the slaughter."

Owen didn't need asking twice.

***

Cyril was sitting in Julie's office at the God forsaken hour of 04:30. He had little enthusiasm for the jarred specimens, he was having a fierce battle with his eyelids and they were beginning to sense victory. Julie burst through the door, a dynamo of energy.

"At least you've been to bed, Bennett; get a grip, man!"

Cyril forced his eyes wide open and then smiled.

"Carla Bonhomme, thirty-two years old, no sign of recent drug or alcohol intake. Died from a cervical fracture, severe twist to the right suggesting a left-handed person with either great strength or training, more than likely both. No other external visible damage other than bruising to her chin and right wrist. Liver mortis shows that she was initially left in a seated position, probably a car seat as there is pooling around the ankles and buttocks. If it's any consolation she didn't suffer!"

Cyril tried to hold back a yawn but failed miserably. "Sorry!"

"This should wake you!" She tossed three scan disks across the table.

Cyril leaned over to pick them up.

"Found in her vagina. All three top quality and high memory."

His hand hovered over the objects and then was retracted quickly.

She chuckled before turning the laptop screen round. "We've checked them. They were secure in a condom; they'll not give you an STI! She had placed them there herself of that I've no doubt."

Cyril watched as the room he had seen many times before, the masks and the coloured girls appeared on screen. Julie wound it on until a blonde man dragged in a white female.

"Pause please. That's Karen Johnson."

"When I start this section watch the technique."

Cyril twitched as Charles turned Karen round, bringing her to stand in front of him. His hands moved quickly and he positioned one on her chin whilst the other wrapped around the back of her head. There was a swift push and then a whip-like pull. The girl simply fell at his feet. Charles merely lifted his arms and stepped backwards in readiness for the bladder and bowel release. He looked down in disgust then left the room.

Julie changed the disk and ran the next. "These are not the same quality they were taken more candidly."

Cyril watched as the images showed the outside of the buildings and a view into the distance. He was now on high alert as excitement flushed through his body, at last they had a clue as to where Liz might be held. For the first time in a number of days, he had hope, a hope that they would find her alive.

"Thank you so very much." He leaned over and covered Julie's hand. "It shouldn't be difficult to find this location."

"We've uplifted these disks to your system."

Cyril called Newby Wiske to confirm that the films had been received. They had and the location had been identified. Two teams of Special Firearms' Officers would be in position within the half hour. DI Podmore had organised the teams in readiness for a pre dawn search. Cyril then called Owen before he rushed to Pateley Bridge. He left the siren off but had the blue strobes on. Within twenty-five minutes he was turning into the car park. He ran to the control unit.

Owen was already there, sipping coffee. He looked at Cyril and for the first time ever, he noticed that he had not shaved.

"Where's the location?" Cyril controlled his breathing.

Owen stood and looked at the Ordinance Survey Map on the board. "We're here and the farm is Telfor's Brook… there. There's a long track, tree lined, but there's little cover except for the darkness as you approach the farm buildings from any other direction. There's a group there now reconnoitring. We have a clear satellite image of the farm and the buildings. Each building has been numbered and each will be cleared in turn. They've reported that there are lights on in the main building and a light in one of the barns. There are two vehicles in the courtyard. Sensory lights surrounding the periphery but no dogs or geese have been seen or heard. The live images are here." Owen pointed to a screen showing the green-hazy night camera images.

"We plan to close the track as the two firearms' teams move in from either side, all with night vision. Two radios as standard. We'll monitor from the bottom of the track with command here. Paramedics and a doctor are standing by and will be ready as well as the SOCO team. The road linking the farm track will be closed at Pateley and at Ramsgill. Wath Road will also be closed. The time now is 05:22. We'll all move at 05:50 on the command."

The message was sent and they left for the vehicles. Some had already started out. Cyril sat with Owen and Peg watching the clock on the dashboard. They could hear the radio; each had an earpiece. Communications between the Firearms' Unit was on a separate system but the information was patched through. The simple word 'Go' put everyone immediately on a high state of alert.

Within five minutes, contact was established.

"Main farmhouse clear."

There was a pause. "Building one, clear. Building two, clear."

After four minutes the final building, five, was announced clear. There had been four arrests, two females and two males. Cyril looked at Owen, and lifted his hands; he had his fingers crossed.

"Let's hope one of them is our Liz."

Cyril drove up the farm track followed by the paramedics and the SOCO team. Once in the courtyard, the firearms' teams bagged their weapons for checking and the different buildings were taped. Cyril went immediately to the four people who had been in the buildings; none was Liz. His disappointment was palpable. He leaned against one of the walls as the numerous people carried out their various tasks. One of the officers approached.

"We've a cadaver dog on standby; they'll check through the buildings first and then the immediate surroundings. We're expecting at least one body, that of Karen Johnson."

Within forty minutes, the dog had pinpointed a stable block and bed as the resting place of a corpse; it also located the farm trailer and had started tracking to a specific area of the farm. Another ten minutes and the dog had located the shallow grave housing Karen Johnson and Dan Rowney. There was nothing else.

Cyril stood at the entrance to the farm and stared at the lights of Pateley Bridge in the distance. He then scanned the valley, tracking along the lower road until his eyes fell on the dark patch that was Gouthwaite Reservoir. He looked again to the east. The deep black of the sky was slowly lightening and horizontal cracks appeared in the lower levels, adding red and orange to the scene. "Red sky in the morning!" he whispered to himself as a grey mist hung in the valley bottom like a shroud.

The vapour from his cigarette blended with his breath. There was nothing further to be done here. Hopefully Liz's DNA would be found and the search would continue.

Chapter Twenty

The farm track was sealed, but the road leading from Pateley Bridge to Lofthouse and Masham beyond had been opened. Cyril was soon back in the car park. He needed a minute to clear his head. He walked through the gates, crossed the road and entered the park. The river could be heard hidden in the mist. He neither felt the cold nor cared. He simply stared at the War Memorial standing alone on the slight mound of earth. He wasn't a religious man, some might say that he had little faith but they were wrong; he just found his god in different forms. To Cyril there was nothing more sacred than a young child, a setting sun, a beautiful painting; each had the touch of a higher being.

He stood at the crossing as three early cyclists rode towards the village, their bright Lycra clothing contrasting with the morning grey. They moved at speed and as one, travelling over the bridge and then up the High Street. Since the Tour de France and the Tour de Yorkshire, it seemed that everyone had bought a cycle and bright clothing. He sometimes wished he too had a more physical hobby. His morning reveille came in the form of his ring tone; he let it ring for a moment and then answered.

"Bennett."

He listened intensely. "I'm on my way."

He paused as two police vehicles, with their lights flashing blue and sirens cracking the morning air, headed back towards Wath. Checking the road, he ran into the car park. Owen was ready and the car drew towards the entrance.

The narrow, valley road made the speeding vehicle sway, Cyril held the grab handle above the door with his left hand, his right gripped the side of the seat. Soon they passed the small bridge that led to The Farmer's Arms then swept left and travelled the edge of the reservoir, now bright, a morning sky mirror, flat and motionless.

Owen slowed as he approached an area where the road climbed, leaving the water below. Pine trees clung to the left side bringing back darkness and a possible wet, slippery surface.

Once clear, Owen accelerated. The two cars were soon just ahead and Cyril's stomach had moved closer to his neck. Beads of sweat appeared on his forehead as the early signs of motion sickness took hold. To his relief, Ramsgill church appeared to be directly ahead before the road swung left again. On seeing the brake lights, Cyril breathed deeply, the worst of the drive was over.

The cars were directed onto the narrow gravel lanes just past the church. Tape ran across the road between the telephone box and the red GPO letterbox. Cyril and Owen approached the entrance to St Mary's Church, Ramsgill. The wrought iron gate was ajar. Cyril noticed the blue and white tape hanging between trees and gravestones protecting the scene. It was then that he saw her feet. He stopped, the gravel's crunch stopping too. It was either the car journey or the thought of what he was about to witness that made Cyril turn and vomit onto the path. He dug in his pocket for his handkerchief.

"You don't have to see this, Sir, I can do it."

Cyril looked at Owen appreciating the depth of their partnership. He forced a smile to his face as if in defiance of his emotions. He walked forward and looked at the door to the church. He took a deep breath before turning round to look at the body.

The grey, lichen-mottled gravestone on which the corpse rested leaned back slightly, giving the impression that Liz was only sleeping. She was child-like and vulnerable. The grey white coverall showed the same staining as he had seen on the videos. He focused on her hands, small and delicate, each resting on the grass at either side. He crouched lower desperate to see her face.

It was then that he noticed it, positioned just to the left of the zip. It was another red-brown mark, another patch of dried blood. Something caught the light, set in a crease of the material at the centre of the stain. The elaborate tip of a Charles Horner pin was sunk deep into her chest.

He closed his eyes and whispered the word *sorry* over and over again.

Time seemed to stand still as he closed his eyes to rid himself of the dreadful image. He heard Owen cough and he looked again at Liz. His tear-filled eyes then focused on the gravestone's inscription that was to the right of her shoulder:

'Remember me as you pass by
As you are now so once was I
As I am now so you must be
Prepare yourself to follow me.'

Cyril turned away unable to control his emotions and he sobbed, collapsing to the ground.

Owen moved closer and wrapped an arm around Cyril's shoulders and squeezed. The only other officer looked away, he too overcome by the outpouring of grief.

"Look what I've done! He wanted me! He wanted me! Why not kill me?"

"Come on, Sir, don't talk like that, not here, not in front of Liz. She wouldn't want you here to see her like this. She'd want you to remember her as she was, as we knew her. She'd want you to be strong. It's not your fault."

Owen helped Cyril to his feet and they walked back the way they had come. Owen stopped at the gate, allowing Cyril to move onto the road alone. He kept a respectful distance behind, but a close eye on his grieving colleague. He could see the rise and fall of Cyril's shoulders, the pain was drawn from deep within. Cyril stopped at the car and wiped his face. He looked up, saw Peg approaching and turned to look away; he was a mess. Through watery eyes, he saw that two cyclists had stopped just past the police car that was positioned as a roadblock at the far side of the tape. They had seen Cyril leave the church and had watched his distress, His stomach churned again.

Peg rested a hand on his shoulder. "I'm so sorry, Sir. Do you want me to organise this?"

He shook his head. "Liz wouldn't have given up, she'd have just got on with the job. I can at least do that for her. I need a minute though and I'll be fine. It's Owen's bloody driving, thinks he's Stirling Moss." He tried to lighten his mood and give them some assurance that he had his emotions under control.

He walked up slowly towards the phone box. He wanted to instruct the officer to keep the area sealed off until Forensics had checked it out. He ducked under the tape.

"Is she one of ours, Sir? One of the lads said she might be."

Cyril simply nodded and looked at his feet. The vomit had spattered his shoes and the bottom of his trousers; an intense anger stirred within him. It was then he spied it, just away from the grassy kerb.

"What's that?" Cyril pointed to the road.

The officer walked towards it.

"Don't touch it!" Cyril ordered. His firm, raised voice made his colleague stop in his tracks.

Cyril walked over and bent down. It was a bicycle spoke. He took a glove from his pocket and picked it up. He walked slowly back to Owen, holding it out.

"It's a spoke."

"*Are broken spokes in the great wheel of good which shall in due time be made whole?* Get in the car! This road leads to Lofthouse with a turn to Middlesmoor which I know is a dead end. Get a patrol car to block the road at the top of Trapping Hill, the road that leads from Lofthouse. I want it at the top."

Cyril's mood had quickly changed, causing Owen some concern. He had read how the death of someone close could affect a person's actions. "Now I want you to sit there." He then pointed to the passenger seat. "Peg's going to take charge. We're going for a gentle drive."

Owen looked at Cyril and then at Peg. Clearly confused, Peg just nodded at Owen and mouthed, 'go'. He did as requested. Cyril stopped the car by the tape as it was removed, then drove steadily on. He said nothing. On arriving at Lofthouse, he turned right out of the village. The stone houses hugged the narrow road until the last two appeared to squeeze the road so narrowly that it seemed that they would not get through. It was on leaving the village that Cyril saw the cyclists struggling with the hill.

"You've not met Charles have you, Owen?"

Owen simply looked at Cyril, convinced that the sight of Liz lying in the churchyard had disturbed his mind. It was at that point that Cyril accelerated. The car lurched forward making a direct line for the cyclists.

"Sir! What the bloody hell are… The bikes!"

It took a moment for Owen to realise what was happening and a split second for him to react. He leaned over and grabbed and turned the steering wheel violently.

"Owen, No!"

The strength of Owen's one hand was easily a match for Cyril's determined grip. The car swerved violently, but not enough to prevent the two cyclists colliding heavily with the front wing of the car. The sound of bending metal, reverberated within. The first cyclist to be hit took the full impact and literally flew into the air, quickly followed by what was left of his bicycle.

Cyril stamped on the brake and the car slid along the road before mounting the grass verge. Within seconds, Cyril was out of the car and running down the grassy bank towards the prostrate figures. Owen followed.

Watching Cyril move swiftly towards the bigger of the two riders, Owen went instinctively to the other who was now beginning to sit up. Blood ran from his nose and from a cut above his right eye. Owen's attention was drawn to the other figure by the scream that shattered the air. He looked across and saw Cyril hovering over him. He moved across swiftly, concerned at the commotion. He could see immediately that the man's leg was bent at an angle that suggested it was badly broken. To his amazement, he saw Cyril raise his foot before planting it directly onto the damaged leg. The scream was intense. Cyril turned to Owen.

"Owen, meet the bastard, Charles." He pressed his weight down again. "You found and killed the Shylocks and the Judases but we have finally found the Devil."

Owen's face was wracked with confusion as he moved towards the prostrate figure.

"He's Charles? How? Why is he here?"

It was then that he noticed the blonde hair. Cyril raised his leg and applied a little pressure onto the disfigured limb until Charles's scream ceased and he lost consciousness. He then looked at the other cyclist who was trying to get to his feet.

"Now who the hell are you?" Bennett said with a degree of venom as he approached the other cyclist.

"Please don't hurt him, Sir!"

Owen was already making a call to Control.

Epilogue

Cyril poured the remaining drops from the second bottle of white wine. The waitress hovered, hoping that he would pay and leave. The bill had been placed on his table fifteen minutes earlier and he was the last customer for the afternoon shift.

The temperature had fallen considerably during the afternoon; Cyril wrapped his scarf more tightly around his neck and paid the bill. He crossed the road and headed for the station to catch the train to Wihr au Val. The small station building, a yellow brick pre-war structure, was immaculate. He checked the clock that sat high above the main entrance. He had a twenty-minute wait. Being in France, a different country, a different culture, enabled him to feel insulated. Whether it was the climate, the mountains, the different language or simply the numbing effect of the wine, it all helped to shield him from his crippling guilt.

The train journey was short and he stood, watching the fields pass. He was soon leaving Wihr au Val station. He failed to notice the person sitting on the station bench, huddled and wrapped. He crossed the main road and walked up Rue de la Gare before stopping at the narrow bridge that ran over the River Fecht. It immediately brought to mind the river at Pateley Bridge; the size of the waterway was the same as the Nidd, so too was its clarity and its colour; it was tree lined and secretive. He let the sound of the tumbling water fill his confused mind as tears ran down his cheeks, falling and blending with the water below before being carried away; if only his guilt could be washed clean, dissolved and lost as easily. The day was quickly drawing to a close.

He thought of the last moments of his investigation. He could see the two cyclists struggling along the steep, narrow lane and then the collision. Had Owen not turned the wheel at the last moment he would have killed one if not both men. He wished now that he had, at least he would have taken an eye for an eye.

The clinical audacity that Charles had demonstrated, his blatant disregard, casually spectating his grief angered him. To design and then mock his professional nadir he could not and would not forgive. Had he not left the cemetery quickly following his breakdown on seeing Liz, he would not have seen the two of them, they would have disappeared. They would have enjoyed seeing his heartbreak but would have then casually left in plain sight leaving the spoke to be discovered by the SOCOs after they were long gone. It would have been like a final nail that they hammered into his conscience for him to battle with. By pure chance, he had seen them and he would happily have killed them with his bare hands, as, he was convinced, would have Owen.

Atkins's plaintive cry not to hurt Charles was a conundrum. Both he and Owen had been shocked when they had realised who he was.

The figure who had watched him get off the train now stood across the main road close to the trees, staring at the lonely man, waiting for the right moment.

On questioning, it was discovered that Atkins had not been hiding family skeletons, covering for his sister's death all that time. Yes, Valerie had pushed Jennifer to her death and he had threatened to tell if she did not tow the line. He manipulated her, threatened and blackmailed her, but that was only until she had discovered his passion for boys; then the tables had been swiftly turned. He became subservient and withdrawn until they both went to university. It was there that she had met an acquaintance of Charles's and then Charles himself. When they were both back home, she had taken James to a party where he and Charles first met. Their developing relationship was flexible but it continued with James even visiting Charles at his home in the South of

France on numerous occasions. James also had been made aware of Val's voracious sexual appetite and had witnessed her gradual drug dependency; the tables had again begun to turn. It was then that she met John, James' best friend, but she had soon sullied that relationship by mentioning her brother's sexuality. The friendship quickly deteriorated with threats levelled on both sides: James was the one to bend. He ran.

It was only on the surprise receipt of Valerie's laptop that James had become fully aware of Charles's activities. James then had a choice to make. Did he support the man that he loved, or did he support the memory of the dead sister he loathed and the man who had shown little sensitivity towards him? According to James, who was guilty of withholding crucial evidence, the decision had been an easy one. Charles had been the only person to accept him for what he was. To Cyril, he should be hung out to dry and Charles? He would gladly do to him what he had done to Liz.

Cyril took one more look over the bridge. The darkness had swallowed the light. He set off towards his hotel.

The figure crossed the road; the day's light was fast diminishing.

"Cyril Bennett! DCI Cyril Bennett!"

Cyril stopped dead hearing his name called. He had left his title back in Yorkshire days before and did not want to hear it again until he was ready, if ever. A shiver ran down his neck. He turned slowly and looked back towards the bridge and into the gloom.

"A penny for all your thoughts, Cyril."

The figure moved slowly towards him, hand outstretched. Of all the people he would want to see, this was the one. He walked quickly back towards her and they embraced.

"Julie… how? Where did you come from?"

"They told me at the hotel that you'd walked into Munster and that you were intending to get the train back. I waited on the platform." She kissed him on the lips and smelled the sweet wine on his breath.

Tears again began to stream down his cheeks as he rested his forehead on hers. His shoulders lifted involuntarily as he sobbed.

"We have the time to rebuild, Cyril. We cannot bring Liz back, but we can honour her memory by upholding what she truly believed in and that's fighting crime and keeping Harrogate safe from the likes of Charles."

He wiped his face on his sleeve and she chuckled.

"If David Owen saw this Cyril Bennett, he'd never let you live it down."

Cyril tried to smile.

"You've been fighting an unseen enemy, all of you and you've won, Liz and the team, they won. Honour the victory and honour her. They are naming a wing in the new North Yorkshire Police Headquarters after Liz, The Liz Graydon Suite. Remember, my brave man, that she died doing a job she loved, she died defending the people she loved and if she had a choice..."

Julie linked Cyril's arm as they walked from the dark towards the few lights of Wihr au Val.

Acknowledgements

It is hard to believe that this is the conclusion of DCI Cyril Bennett's fourth case. He and the rest of the team have now become a firm part of my family. It was a difficult decision to plot Liz's demise and one that I didn't take lightly, but sometimes life deals devastating blows that make each and every one of us take stock and re-think our position in life.

Writing is such a pleasure but one that, for me, requires a good deal of support. Although I type the words there are many people who, through their various skills, help form and wreak the raw material into a tangible structure. I must offer a massive thanks to the wonderful team at Bloodhound Books, the editors, the cover designers and all those beavering away behind the scenes. I shall be ever grateful to Betsy and Fred for having faith in my writing. They are the ticking heart of Bloodhound.

To Helen Claire, Kerry-Ann Richardson for their support for me as a newly published writer, it made a difference. Thank you.

I am constantly humbled by the support received from the many bloggers who promote indie writers. Please keep doing what you do so well.

A big thanks to a number of groups: Crime Fiction Addict, TBC, UK Crime Club and Crime Book Club on Facebook. Your support is so valued.

I am blessed in having a dedicated group of readers who are always there to offer honest, critical insights into my work. To Stuart, Chris, Margaret, Bill, Barbara, Tony, Eileen and Peter, my sincere thanks.

To Carrie, who always casts a critical eye over the second draft, your patience is appreciated.

To my wife, Debbie, without you I'd be nothing. X

Last, but certainly not least, I have to thank you, the reader. Thank you for your continued support.

Malcolm

"There are moments when I feel that the Shylocks, the Judases, and even the Devil are broken spokes in the great wheel of good which shall in due time be made whole."
Helen Keller. 'The Story of My Life'

Lightning Source UK Ltd.
Milton Keynes UK
UKOW04f0609041017
310352UK00001B/114/P